My Darcy Mutates...

A Collection of
Pride and Prejudice-inspired
steamy short stories

by

ENID WILSON

To

All my online fans. You give me inspiration!

Enid Wilson loves sexy romance. Her writing career began with a daily newspaper, writing educational advice for students. She then branched out into writing marketing materials and advertising copy.

Enid's novels, *In Quest of Theta Magic*, *Bargain with the Devil* and *Really Angelic*, received several top reviews. *Bargain with the Devil* has been ranked in the top 50 best-selling historical romances on Amazon USA, while *Really Angelic* in the top 30 best-selling Regency romances on Amazon Canada.

Enid loves to hear from her readers. You can contact her at enid.wilson28@yahoo.com.au or www.steamydarcy.com

Illustrations and cover design by Z. Diaz

First published 2010

Historical

Fantasy

Modern

Historical

What if old Mr. Darcy was still alive…

APOLLO'S STONE

"Explain to me, my love, how this great scheme of yours will work," the woman asked huskily as she caressed the man's hips.

"The spoiled brat and I will ride ahead. We will arrive here as planned. I shall endeavour to have all three unsuspecting men deep in their cups. Then I shall personally see to his retirement to the designated chamber and let him know that I have arranged for a sensual woman for his enjoyment. From the last experience, I know that he reacted most amorously when he was given this particular type of Scottish whisky.

"At the same time, a friend of mine will overturn a cart on the road to Meryton, thus delaying his father's carriage for a few hours. Once his father arrives, some commotion will be created, and I shall bring the old goat in. You can scream about the drunkard bastard dragging you into a guest chamber and imposing on you." The young man gave a sly grin. "The old man will pay a fortune to keep your mouth shut, once he happens upon you and his son in all your glory, with witnesses in tow."

"Do I get to sample the magnificent body of Fitzwilliam Darcy?" she asked, and licked her lips eagerly.

The man pinched her nipple. "I am ten times more glorious than he. But if you want us to witness his dismal attempt to satisfy you, then go to it, by all means." He rolled the woman over and thrust into her. "In fact, that is a fine idea. Let him spend his seed in you." He pushed in and out with mechanical precision, while the lady moaned in high pitch. When he reached the moment of satisfaction, he did not pull out as he usually did, but spilled his fluid into her. "We will pass my child off as his, and the old goat will keep the money rolling in at our door."

"Yes!" the woman cried. "Excellent idea!"

***

Caroline Bingley was extremely annoyed with herself. Whatever had prompted her to invite Jane Bennet to Netherfield, two days ago? On further thought, however, she told herself she should not be angry with herself but with that stupid girl. Who else would have ridden across three miles of open roads in heavy rain? Was her family truly so poor that they could not afford a carriage?

Indeed, it appeared to be true that the Bennets could not spare a carriage, because her sister Eliza had arrived on foot, as well, the day before. Why had she felt compelled to trudge around the countryside, all alone on muddy lanes for hours, just because her sister had a cold? *Perhaps both of them have designs on Charles*, Caroline thought. And it was past annoying that idiot brother of hers had invited both of them to stay until Miss Bennet recovered.

Her scheme would be hindered with two strangers in the house. Mr. Fitzwilliam Darcy and his father would arrive later in the day. *Perhaps I should make Miss Eliza sick, as well, to ensure that she will not get in the way. Yes, that is a brilliant idea.*

***

When Miss Elizabeth Bennet sent word that she would not join the host family for breakfast because her sister was still rather sick, Miss Bingley was seen personally taking a tray to the sick room, around noontime.

As Miss Bennet had fallen asleep, Miss Bingley stayed on to take some refreshment with Miss Eliza. She then urged her guest to drink a cup of warm tea in which she had mixed some liquor and a drop of laudanum, observed covertly with keen eyes until her guest had finished all of the drink. To her gratified amazement, Miss Eliza seemed to become both giddy and sleepy.

Miss Bingley asked Miss Eliza if she wished to retire for the day, and the latter agreed. With wobbly legs, the guest excused herself and stumbled out of her sister's room to walk haphazardly along the corridor, freeing Miss Bingley to start down the stairs, filled with smug contentment.

In the meantime, the dazed young lady walked on until she reached a room which she thought to be hers, whereupon she pushed the door open and toppled onto the bed almost immediately. The curtain was drawn and the room was dark.

Not caring whether Eliza was well settled or not, Caroline rushed away to make preparations for her important guests. She now believed that the problem of Miss Eliza was solved. That importunate young woman would be in no condition to interfere with her scheme.

At two in the afternoon, her other guests arrived. After they were shown to their rooms and had refreshed themselves, they joined the host family in the sitting room.

"Mr. Darcy, welcome to Netherfield." Miss Bingley batted her lashes and greeted him in her most elegant tones. "But wherever is your esteemed father?"

"Thank you, Miss Bingley. Mr. Wickham and I rode ahead of my father's carriage. You have met my father's godson, George Wickham?" Darcy inquired.

"Darce, it is good to have you in Netherfield. Mr. Wickham, welcome." Charles Bingley shook their hands warmly. "What do you think of it?"

"It is of good size. The house looks fine and the countryside pretty. You did well in leasing it," Darcy replied whole-heartedly.

The gentlemen discussed the hunting activities in Hertfordshire for some minutes.

"Charles, perhaps you would like to retreat to the study with the gentlemen. I shall let you know when the senior Mr. Darcy's carriage arrives," Mrs. Louisa Hurst suggested.

"Excellent!" George Wickham agreed. He clapped the back of Mr. Hurst in a friendly manner and urged the men away.

Mr. Darcy did not care to spend time with Wickham, but his father took his duty as his godfather seriously, and so he vowed to be as polite as he could.

Caroline threw her fan on the couch and said to her sister angrily, "What was that for? Why did you urge the men out of the room so soon?"

"Caroline, you must desist. Did you not see that he is not interested in you?" Louisa replied.

"I see no such thing." Caroline retorted. "I am smart, elegant and fashionable. Why would he not be interested in me?"

Lousia shook her head and said, "I am saying this only for your good. But if you intend to capture him while he stays here, you had better go and rest now before preparing for tonight's dinner. You have dark circles under your eyes. Perhaps the noise from the Bennet sisters gave you a restless night?"

"Do I really have black bags under the eyes? Why did you not tell me earlier? It was that impertinent country nobody, Eliza, wandering around the corridor, trying to find the library, late at night." With that, Miss Bingley dashed out of the sitting room and retreated to her own chamber hastily, leaving her sister to shake her head once again.

***

Half an hour later, Mr. Darcy received a note from his father, stating that the carriage had suffered a minor accident a little distance from Meryton. His father would stretch his legs in the small town for the time being, until the carriage was sorted out. He would arrive at Netherfield in another hour.

Soon, Wickham had Mr. Darcy, Mr. Hurst and Mr. Bingley drunk. He left Hurst and Bingley in the study and helped the tipsy Mr. Darcy up the stairs in person, not wanting Darcy's valet to intercept him.

When Wickham arrived at the room he had shared with his lady love, it was almost pitch dark because the curtains were drawn close. A dim light that entered through a gap between the curtains was just enough for him to make out the shape of a woman under the bed sheet. She was lying on her stomach, and her hair was loosened. *She certainly knows how to stay mute*, Wickham thought. *She is determined not to let Fitzwilliam know who she is.*

Wickham started stripping Fitzwilliam of his clothes. "I have a surprise for you," he said to the inebriated gentleman.

"What's…it?" Darcy hiccupped.

"A sensual woman." Turning Darcy, he pointed to the bed.

"With gorgeous… bosom?" The dazed man chuckled.

"Possibly," Wickham said, wondering why Darcy's cravat had to be so complicated. "You'll have to discover that for yourself."

"I have not gotten…laid for some years now," Darcy lamented. "Father keeps…me close and works me hard…ever since you last…got me into mischief…"

"Then what are you waiting for?" Wickham demanded, finally getting the shirt off the half-drunk man.

"She is …willing?" Darcy staggered forward a step.

"Very." Wickham unbuttoned Darcy's breeches.

Darcy hesitated, swaying. "I do not sleep with… whores."

"Her husband is dead," Wickham lied as he stripped the drunken man naked.

"A lonely widow?"

"A most easily aroused one."

"She wants…money from me?" Darcy asked stubbornly, not moving.

"Not at all. She only wants affection and warmth." *Blast the spoiled brat, why did he need to ask so many questions? Damn his standards of refusing to mix with fortune hunters and lowly whores.*

"But…I do not…trust you." Darcy argued. "Are you trying to…trick me? You are always up to…no good."

Wickham swore under his breath. He had no time for Darcy's censure. He shoved the drunkard onto the bed, walked out the door and closed it. *Let her do her job!*

"Ouch!"

"Ah!"

Mr. Darcy and the woman both exclaimed as their bodies crashed onto each other.

"I beg your pardon, Madam." He stood up and bowed awkwardly.

The woman turned over on the bed, had a look at him, laughed and asked cheerily, "Is your apology for ...bumping into me or appearing without a... stitch of clothing, in my bed chamber?"

Darcy liked her sound, musical and pleasant. He smiled and looked down at himself in the muted light. "Indeed, I am in all my glory. I do not...know why."

She sat up, brushed the wayward curls away from her eyes, and took in the sight of his strong frame with apparent curiosity. "You look like a ... statue of the Greek god, Apollo," she said, and hiccupped.

"Your bosom...rivals that of Venus." He licked his lips and felt a sudden surge of heat rise in his body. Intending to let in some air, he walked to pull the curtains wider apart.

She cast a look at herself. Lit by the bright afternoon sun from outside, she saw that she wore no clothes, either. She remembered feeling oppressively hot, shortly after she went to the bed, scarcely able to breathe. Stifling, she had taken her dress off and then, finding little relief, had shed the rest of her garments before surrendering again to sleep. Now, abruptly awakened, she was covered by nothing but the bed sheet which was now pooled at her waist.

"Thank you, Sir, for the compliment." She smiled, feeling giddily light-headed beneath the gaze of this handsome young man. She reclined down on the bed again and raised both hands to rub her temples. "But I am not the goddess of love, but simple Elizabeth Bennet of Longbourn."

Mr. Darcy felt the room grow hotter yet. The lovely Elizabeth was lying on the bed, with both hands on her forehead, a gesture which pushed her gorgeous breasts higher still. She had the most vivid green eyes, a very fine pair. He wanted to worship her but was not sure whether she would welcome it. He was a gentleman and would never force himself on a woman. The temptation was so great that he felt as if his head might burst at any moment.

He raised his hand to rub his own temple.

"Are you…not feeling well, Apollo?" she asked with concern.

"I am no Apollo, just Fitzwilliam Darcy…of Pemberley."

"Perhaps you will feel better if you lie down," she suggested, and patted the space beside her.

It was an invitation he could not refuse. He slipped in besides her, under the bed sheet.

They stared at each other silently for a minute. Then she smiled at him and raised her eyebrows. Encouraged, he stretched out his hand and touched her, drawing delicate circles around one of her nipples.

The cherry tip peaked and she gasped for air.

"You have the most … magic touch," she murmured.

"And you are very… responsive."

She smiled widely at his compliment. The whole-hearted grin made her look fresh and carefree, like his sister

Georgiana, Mr. Darcy thought. Elizabeth seemed too young to have been married and then widowed. But what did he really know about such things? Had his own mother not died very young, too, soon after Georgiana was born?

"How old are you?" he asked. His finger continued the exploration of her twin peaks. He loved the texture of her skin.

"Not yet one-and-twenty," she whispered. "And you?"

"Not yet eight-and-twenty."

"In the prime of life." She gazed at his eyes, which were the deepest blue, like the summer sky. He seemed indeed to be a Greek god, calling out for her to touch him. Emboldened, she traced her fingers from his throat down his chest to his navel. His body was virile and perfect.

His mouth gaped open as he felt his skin burn beneath her touch. His arousal sprang up, proud and tall, making a tent of the bed sheet.

Her eyes widened at the unexpected movement. She lifted the edge of the bed sheet, took one quick glance at his magnificent manhood, and dropped the sheet immediately.

"I did not know that Apollo's…stone could grow," she remarked innocently.

He chuckled. "Would you like to feel the stone…expand?" He took her tiny hand, which was soft but surprisingly strong, and placed her fingers around his shaft.

"It is…" She swallowed and bit her lower lip. "It is so hot…and so smooth."

He slid his other hand down to her apex, where he rubbed the soft bush and slid along her folds. "And you are wet and…blazing."

She could feel the blood draining from her head, seeming to pool and pulse at her sex. The sensations at the juncture of her thighs were raging, causing her to flex her hand instinctively, squeezing his shaft hard.

He let out a cry of pure ecstasy. He knew that he would explode if he did not join with this lovely Venus.

Carefully, he removed her hand from his straining member, then turned to press his body against her. The moment their naked forms touched, they both shivered. Using his elbows to carry his weight, he positioned himself over her and lowered his head to kiss her sultry lips with passion.

When he thrust his tongue into her mouth, she sucked at it tentatively, and her sweet response nearly made him come. He pulled back immediately and lowered his lips to worship her creamy mounds instead.

They were alabaster white, soft and bouncy. He licked the skin around the nipples, then moved to the side once again and took his weight upon a single elbow in order to free one hand to shape her bountiful hips. Enchanted, he paused between each lick to tell her how beautiful she looked. In answer, she moaned in pleasure and buried her fingertips in his hair.

As he suckled her nipples soundly for several long minutes, her soul seemed to draw up and out of her body. She rolled her eyes, twisted her body and, with a final sweet convulsion, reached Heaven. The juice of climax flew out from her secret lips.

Rising over her in earnest, he nudged her thighs apart and used his hand to position his shaft. Insinuating his manhood between her nether lips, he found that she was tight, even with the sweetness of her essence. Bracing himself, he bore down, pushing slowly into her.

The sensation was unexplainable as his tip was swallowed up, a fraction of an inch at a time, by this hot volcano. Bearing down, he thrust with his rigid rod, determined to penetrate into the very heart of her core.

All the while, her inner muscles teased and squeezed and clenched, bombarding him with maddening sensation. Her body seemed to mock his ardor, refusing to yield further. Delirious with desire, he grasped her thighs and pulled them even wider apart, then plunged forward, using every bit of leverage he could muster to break through all barriers, the better to merge with her.

Beneath him, she screamed out in pain.

He froze, stunned, then raised his head as comprehension dawned upon him. "You are a maiden?" he whispered hoarsely.

Elizabeth panted and shifted beneath him, unshed tears brightening her beautiful eyes. "Yes…and I find…your stone…very hard, Apollo."

A part of him wanted to laugh, touched by the gallant courage of her remark, but her movements were reigniting him. With his hands and mouth, he pleasured her breasts with a determined eagerness, while he exerted all his will power to hold his lower body still.

When she was once again aroused to unbearable heights, and began to twist and squirm beneath him, he withdrew himself almost to her entrance and then thrust into her again in a smooth, heated glide.

Once started, he could not stop. His pace soon grew fast, urgent and lustful. He drove into her like a stud covering a spirited mare, aiming to conquer and to please.

Sweat drenched both of their bodies. She clawed at his muscular back as he pounded into her. The slick sound of his thighs smacking against hers was accompanied by her ever-louder moans. His hands and mouth were merciless, nipping and rubbing her nipples and lips, exciting her to new sensory heights.

Lost in this new world of sensual desperation, she cried out his name, "Fitzwilliam!" several times, until at last the world exploded behind her eyes in a torrent of delight, and he cried out as well, flooding her with his essence.

Finally, descending from their cosmic peak, they returned to earth. Pulling the bed sheet up to cover their satiated bodies, he embraced her tightly, and they drifted off to sleep.

Within a few minutes, however, the door was opened by George Wickham, accompanied by old Mr. Darcy. Miss Bingley was hot on their heels.

"I thought I heard Fitzwilliam here…" Wickham said, then faltered into silence as he blinked his eyes, adjusting to the unexpected brightness of the room.

Pushing past him, Miss Bingley screamed in fury. "Eliza Bennet, you shameless, penniless chit! What have you done to *my* Mr. Darcy?"

The disturbance woke the couple in the bed. At that moment, Louisa Hurst opened the servant's entrance to the room, dressed in a nearly transparent nightgown, her loosened hair tumbled about her shoulders. She took one startled look at the commotion, gasped, and fled the room immediately.

Elizabeth shook her head in an attempt to clear the last lingering effects of the liquor and the drug from her body. She blinked up at the two strange men, one young, one old, who stood with Miss Bingley. Then she noticed a subtle movement by her side. A man was sleeping there, his bare body pressed intimately to hers. She was ready to scream and flee the bed…but she found that she was no longer wearing anything at all.

"What have you done to me?" she demanded of the young man holding her.

Mr. Darcy shook his head and looked up at the lovely vision besides him, remembering the incredible love making that had occurred between them just minutes before. His mind no longer seemed to be dulled by the alcohol so much. But the accusing expressions of the onlookers made him felt guilty. "I am sorry, Father. I was drunk."

Old Mr. Darcy breathed deeply and asked Mr. Wickham and Miss Bingley to leave the room.

As Elizabeth began to remember what had happened, through the haze of cloud that still filled her head, she burst into tears, and murmured, "How could this have happened? One minute, I was drinking tea with Miss Bingley, and the next minute I felt giddy and so very drowsy. I was sleeping here, all by myself. Why did you come in? What have you done?"

"Do not cry, child," Old Mr. Darcy said kindly. "I shall step out for just a minute. The two of you must rise and dress. I know that it is highly improper to question you here and now, but I want to get to the bottom of this, without delay."

As soon as the old gentleman went out into the hallway, Elizabeth and Fitzwilliam dressed quickly, in complete silence, without looking at each other. When Elizabeth sat down again upon the bed, he opened the door for his father.

Old Mr. Darcy began the questioning. "My name is George Darcy, and this is my son, Fitzwilliam Darcy. What is your name?"

"Elizabeth Bennet, Sir."

"Of the Bennets of Longbourn? Amazing. I met your father this very day, while my carriage was being repaired at Meryton. Your father's estate is quite nearby."

Elizabeth nodded.

"You are a guest here?"

"Yes, sir. My sister Jane became ill while she was visiting Miss Bingley, two days ago. I came, yesterday, to take care of her. Mr. Bingley invited me to stay on until Jane was better."

"And you mentioned feeling giddy and sleepy after drinking some tea?"

"Yes, actually. Jane was quite sick, this morning, so I told Miss Bingley that I would not go down for breakfast. She brought me some refreshments and tea personally around noontime. It was very kind of her, but after I drank it, I felt quite strange, and so I went to my..." She looked around uncertainly. "I did not know how I got here. This is not the guest room where I stayed, last night."

"That is strange." Young Darcy frowned. "Miss Bingley is not…"

"…known for her kindness," Old Mr. Darcy completed the sentence, and shared a candid glance with his son.

"I was rather surprised, too, sir," Elizabeth added. "Ever since Miss Bingley learned that we have little dowry, with our estate entailed away to a male cousin, and our uncle in trade and living in Cheapside, she has been… Well, in truth, sir, she has of late been rather rude to Jane and me."

Old Mr. Darcy stepped outside again, and called for his valet to check with a maid and have the cups and cutlery used for refreshments from Miss Bennet's room brought to him discreetly. He then returned to the silent room and turned to his son with a stern expression. "And you, son. How do you come to be here."

"George, Charles, Hurst and I were drinking in the study while we waited for you. George had this special Scottish whisky that he insisted that we sample. I knew that

I should not, but…I did. And I fear that I got drunk quite quickly, just like the last time."

"Like the last time?" The senior frowned.

"Umh, yes. When I was around three-and-twenty. Wickham and I sampled that same brand of whisky in a tavern when we were at Cambridge." Fitzwilliam's face turned bright red. He had later heard that he started singing love songs and dancing on the table, wanted to kiss every one and take off his clothes. Luckily, a friend prevented him.

"Ah that incident." Old Mr. Darcy nodded. "But how did you come to this bedchamber?"

"I cannot remember clearly. George accompanied me here. He said that…that…" Fitzwilliam stammered to a halt.

"What did he say?" his father demanded.

"He said that he had procured…" He turned to glance at the distraught young lady. "…a sensual widow for my…enjoyment." He lowered his head, not daring to look at his father or the lovely lady.

"I am no widow!" Elizabeth gasped. "I am still a maiden." Tears rolled down her pale cheeks again. "At least, I was, until…"

"I am sorry, Miss Bennet," Mr. Darcy said wretchedly. "Sir, I am sorry. I should have stopped as soon as I realized that she was …untouched. But I did not." He drew in a deep breath, expecting the harshest censure from his father…but his father appeared to be deep in thought. So he walked, instead, to kneel before Elizabeth, his eyes begging for forgiveness. "Miss Bennet, I am deeply sorry for my drunken behaviour. I have compromised you. We must marry."

"But I do not even know you!" she replied in alarm. "What if you are…witless?"

He shook his head. "I completed Cambridge with honours."

"Unkind?"

"I have never raised my hand or voice against a defenceless servant. Our housekeeper, Mrs. Reynolds, can confirm that. She has known me since I was four."

"A gambler?"

"My fortune is still quite intact, at six thousand so far. You may rest assured that I am not a gambler."

She gasped at his wealth, but pressed on, for it was of no true consequence in the present burning matter. Instead, she continued. "A drunkard?"

"I shall have to prove myself to you on that score. I do not usually get drunk. But this one special Scottish whisky does appear to have a most peculiar effect upon me. I vow hereafter to stay away from it entirely."

"But…I want to marry for love." She wanted desperately to look away from the handsome man in front of her, but her eyes betrayed her, for they would not leave his face.

Mr. Darcy sucked in a deep breath and was about to respond when his father waved him to silence and addressed Elizabeth himself.

"That, my dear young woman, is a rather novel notion. To marry for love. As my son said, he is very rich and you do not have a dowry. Will that not change your mind about the marriage?"

She sighed deeply. "If I cannot respect the man by my side, all the money in the world will not make me happy."

Old Mr. Darcy nodded with approval, and waved his permission for Fitzwilliam to continue to argue his case.

"Well then, Miss Bennet, you have only to tell me how to win your respect and I shall try my hardest to do so. Indeed, I have already begun to respect you quite sincerely. You did not hesitate to tell us of your 'less fortunate' family situation, and you pronounce yourself unwilling to marry me, even though I am quite wealthy. I find that admirable indeed."

Elizabeth blinked in surprise. "You have no objection to my relations? I must confess, my mother and younger sisters are rather silly."

"My aunt, Lady Catherine, is not the most reasonable of relations, either."

"Fitzwilliam!" Old Mr. Darcy chastised his son.

"You seem determined to challenge me, Fitzwilliam," Elizabeth said, then turned crimson, for her accidental use of his Christian name caused her to recall crying out the word in the very throes of passion. She had to admit that this fine young man had a hidden sense of humour, a strong code of honour and the most handsome of physical forms. Perhaps...perhaps she *could* trust him with her future.

Mr. Darcy rubbed the insides of her palms. He loved the way she spoke his name, and the twinkle in her eyes. He shivered with pleasure as he remembered hearing her endearingly cry out his name at the height of their ecstasy...

Now, kneeling before her, he felt hot and pleasantly flustered, anticipating a lifelong enjoyment of this responsive, intelligent and no-nonsense beauty. He had only known her for a very short interlude but he felt a surprising connection with her.

Old Mr. Darcy was happily satisfied with their conversation so far. His son knew that he had done wrong, and was taking responsibility for his actions, upholding his duty and honour. And this young woman, though without connections or wealth, seemed an exceptional find, nothing at all like the regrettable Miss Bingley. He felt confident that Miss Elizabeth Bennet would stand up to – and stand by – her husband, for better or worse.

He left the young couple to talk and stepped out of the room again, where he found his valet waiting. As he had suspected, the cup smelt of laudanum and liquor, solving the mystery of Elizabeth's presence in the room.

As for Fitzwilliam's side of the tale, old Mr. Darcy had a good idea that it was indeed his rakish godson's doing. It was evident from the way Wickham had insisted on showing him where Fitzwilliam was, immediately after he finally arrived at Netherfield. Then Mrs. Hurst had appeared by way of the servant's entrant, most improperly attired. And he had not missed the angry glare that was then shared between Wickham and the married woman.

They planned to compromise my son. But what for? To obtain money from me to shut them up, most likely. But were there two separate plans, or did all three of them, Wickham, Mrs. Hurst and Miss Bingley, work together?

He found, abruptly, that he did not care. He was altogether sick of providing Wickham with a second, a third, nay, countless chances. It seemed that the young man's dissolute ways were fixed. Very well, then. Old Mr. Darcy would wash his hands of Wickham. He would buy his godson a commission to India, and have him shipped off immediately. Nor could they stay longer at Netherfield, either.

With a vigorous torrent of plans in his head, old Mr. Darcy returned to the room, where he found that he had interrupted Fitzwilliam and Elizabeth in a sweet embrace. They broke apart, and he told them of his thoughts.

By the time the Darcys and the Bennet sisters drove to Longbourn, Wickham was on his way to Matlock House in London, under the restraint of two sturdy valets, there to await old Mr. Darcy's nephew Colonel Fitzwilliam's arrangement for his passage to India.

Mr. Bingley was told, gently but firmly, of their suspicions about Miss Bingley's use of the laudanum, and of Mrs. Hurst's scheme with Wickham. A horrified Bingley, after some fierce interrogations, extracted the stories from both sisters. Miss Bingley confessed to the use of the drug but denied any involvement with Mr. Wickham. Mrs. Hurst, in her turn, admitted to the blackmailing scheme. She had been having an affair, on and off, with Wickham for some years. On the day of the scheme, she had spent too much primping and had arrived at the guest chamber too late to enact their scheme.

Sick at heart, Bingley sent them both away, back to Scarborough, after their confessions. Mrs. Hurst did not fall pregnant by Wickham, which was fortunate since her husband separated, unofficially but unequivocally, from her after learning about the affairs and the events of the day.

For his part, Bingley apologised to the Bennets and Darcys most profusely, with obvious sincerity. As a result, the incident did not damage his chance with Jane Bennet or his friendship with Darcy.

Mr. Fitzwilliam Darcy married Miss Elizabeth Bennet some three weeks after the incident at Netherfield. Their pre-marital union did not result in a child. A year and a half later, however, when old Mr. Darcy handed over the full management of Pemberley to his son, Elizabeth gave birth to an heir. Eventually, old Mr. Darcy was kept busy with his five grandsons and two granddaughters from his son Fitzwilliam's marriage to Elizabeth. His daughter Georgiana gave him three grandchildren, as well.

The old gentleman did not move out of Pemberley but remained to see the second generation of Mr. and Mrs. Darcy teasing, arguing, comforting and loving each other.

The young couple had a happy life, despite the strange beginning of their acquaintance. Old Mr. Darcy gained a good friend in Mr. Bennet, who came to visit his favourite daughter at the most unexpected time. Even the once-silly Mrs. Bennet became rather sensible once she had grown older and all of her daughters were well settled.

As matters transpired, Old Mr. Darcy did not once regret sending his godson to India, despite the fact that the latter was never heard from again.

What if Mr. Darcy's second proposal had taken place at Netherfield?

IF SOMEONE DISCOVERS US

Instead of receiving a letter of excuse from his friend, as Elizabeth Bennet half-expected Mr. Bingley to do, he was able to welcome Mr. Fitzwilliam Darcy back to Netherfield just a week after Lady Catherine's visit to Longbourn.

The Bennets were invited to Netherfield for the engagement ball and they stayed afterwards, much to the disgust of Miss Bingley, as her brother did not want his beloved Jane to be 'tired' by the carriage ride, even though Longbourn was a scant three miles away.

As Elizabeth sat by the window in the same room she had occupied during Jane's illness a year ago, her thoughts were with the tall, quiet gentleman staying under the same roof. She could still feel the heat of Mr. Darcy's gaze during their first set of dancing. Her hands had trembled, every time they encountered his.

His hands, by contrast, had remained strong, steady and warm. She did not know whether she had imaged it, but it seemed to her that his thumb had gently stroked her fingers, every time he held her hand. She had breathed in his musky scent when he danced a little too close to her, and felt the air vibrate when his chest almost touched her bosom during the dance. It had given her shivers. Both of them had been so absorbed by the moment that they remained silent for most of the dance.

Elizabeth had no memory of any other gentlemen she danced with, that evening, until Mr. Darcy came back to claim the last dance. Much to the surprise of the locals in Meryton, it was the scandalous waltz. To Elizabeth, it was both heaven and hell. She could feel the blood riot in her body when he wrapped his arm around her waist and her hand touched his shoulder. Due to their height difference, she felt him nearly pulling her off the ground as he whirled her around with unnerving intensity and passion. She was sure she touched his body the whole time they danced together. She felt she floated on a cloud with him.

Yet it was torturous because, although she could inhale his masculine aroma, move with his majestic body, and stare at his soulful eyes, he had not opened his heart to her. The occasion was too public. They had parted, retreating to their respective chambers with only a look of silent longing for each other...

With a deep sigh, Elizabeth rose from the seat and left the elegant guest chamber in Netherfield in search of a book to help her sleep. At the top of the stairs, she gasped and froze as she saw Mr. Darcy walking up. He was without his coat and cravat, and his hair was a bit dishevelled.

Mr. Darcy's legs nearly failed him upon seeing the lovely form of Elizabeth above him. Her long, curly hair streamed down her shoulders. The white nightgown seemed to accentuate every hill and valley of her beautiful body. The moonlight shone through the window behind her, giving her an ethereal aura.

He had just finished consumed a few glasses of port, alone in the library, thinking about their torturous dances, her fragrance and her fine eyes. Now here she was, tempting him again. He breathed deeply and forced his legs to begin climbing again. He had to find out whether she was real.

When he reached the top step of the stair, his eyes were on the same level with hers. He put his hand out and touched her face. Her skin was warm and soft. *Yes, she was real!* As he saw her mouth trembled and her eyes dilated, he moved his thumb to trace the cherry red of her lips.

"Miss Bennet…"

"Mr. Darcy."

Mr. Darcy's face drew near to Elizabeth's, and he uttered his next words with a vulnerability that touched her heart.

"Elizabeth, I… Pray tell me that your opinion of me has changed. My affections and wishes are even more ardent than before. I love you. I could never live happily without you."

Her heart ached for him. She replied immediately, "My opinion…my feelings have indeed changed. I love you. I have loved you since …"

Her declaration was, however, cut short. Mr. Darcy was a man violently in love, one who had just achieved his heart's desire after many months of bitter struggle. He forgot about the sleeping household, the rest of the world, everything but the pure and miraculous fact that Elizabeth Bennet loved him.

His head drew nearer to hers, and he sealed their fate with a kiss.

As kisses go, this one began tenderly. He was tentative at first, unwilling to risk frightening her. As his lips touched hers, however, he felt their very souls intertwine. His love, aspiration and hope for the future were answered in that moment.

Elizabeth's heart was beating so swiftly that she feared it might burst at any moment. She felt the intensity of Mr. Darcy's presence in her whole body. With that kiss, he seemed to have invaded her every pore and nerve. She wetted her lips…no, they were his lips. And just as she thought she could not be closer to him than at that moment, he wrapped his arm around her waist, just as he had done during their waltz. Angling his head slightly, he kissed her even more deeply. They were merged into one, from head to toe.

When they stopped for breath, their eyes shone, and the brightest of smiles adorned their faces.

Elizabeth found herself surprised by his beautiful smile. He looked so happy! Reverting to her impertinent self, she teased, "Mr. Darcy, would you be shocked if I invited you to join me in my chamber? I have a few things to demand from you, and I choose to follow your aunt's advice to use my arts and allurements to make you forget yourself and comply with my wishes."

At such a provocation, his eyes widened. Then he joined her on the landing, passed one arm beneath her legs, and swung her off her feet.

She nearly screamed out, startled by his action. Instead, she chose to wrap her arms around his neck and muffle her cry by pressing her lips to his ear while he bore her off down the hallway toward her room.

***

By the time Elizabeth had thanked Mr. Darcy for his assistance to Lydia, and they expressed their "gratitude" for the interference of Lady Catherine, she had been sitting on his lap for quite some time as they alternated between words and kissing each other on the settee inside her chamber.

"Elizabeth, I think I had better return to my bed chamber before I do something to harm your reputation beyond repair." Mr. Darcy said with a notable lack of conviction as he continued to trace his lips down the neckline of her nightgown.

"If someone discovers us, you shall have to marry me," she said, her hands smoothed over his shoulders and back restlessly, "immediately."

"Yes, immediately!" he echoed as he pushed the nightgown off her shoulders, baring her creamy mounds. She was breathing heavily, causing her delicious breasts to rise and fall dramatically. His heart nearly stopped at the glorious sight, and he devoured her lush bosom with his eyes.

Her nipples hardened under his avid gaze.

He lowered his head and suckled one nipple while his fingers plucked at the other.

Elizabeth felt her body jerk upward, and a hot current sizzled from her breast to her womanhood. She was on fire as Mr. Darcy continued to worship her twin peaks earnestly. Her fingers tore at his hair and dug at his shoulder.

He raised his head and said, "Elizabeth, trust me."

When she had returned his gaze and nodded, he lowered his head and kissed her passionately.

She thought she could not feel any hotter but she was soon proved wrong. She did not know how the hem of her gown had become hiked up, but it had. His hand moved between her thighs, and he began stroking her secret lips.

Elizabeth felt stars burst in her head. As he insinuated one finger into her entrance, her whole body trembled. She moaned and twisted as he slid the finger in and out of her secret garden. As part of his continuing kiss, his tongue mimicked the action of his finger, thrusting into her mouth. Then he introduced a second finger, stretching her muscle slightly, in and out, again and again and again while her breath grew shorter and shorter, until she was suddenly tipped off the edge and reached a climax that caused her to cling to him quite desperately, trembling.

At that, Mr. Darcy stopped his ministration and kisses. His cheek touched hers, and he breathed heavily as he waited for her to still. After he had himself under control, he tidied her clothes and embraced her limp body.

"Elizabeth, my love, I really had better go back to my room now," he said, this time with more conviction.

Elizabeth nodded silently but her eyes were still dark with passion. As he opened the door, she found her strength and flew across the room to clasp him in a tight embrace.

Suddenly, a woman's scream was heard.

Mr. Darcy and Elizabeth both turned towards the sound, which had come from the stairs. As one, they rushed there.

To their horror, Mrs. Hurst lay at the bottom of the stairs, motionless.

More people gathered. A shocked Miss Bingley, Mr. Hurst and their friend, Mr. Willoughby, were all soon gathered at the top of the stairs.

Mr. Darcy was the first to move. He descended the stairs to check on Mrs. Hurst.

"She is alive. Hurst, awaken Bingley and send for the doctor!"

But Mr. Hurst did not move. He seemed frozen. It was Mr. Willoughby who moved, instead, rushing towards the family wing to alert the master of the house.

Mr. Darcy lifted Mrs. Hurst carefully and carried her to her bed chamber, directed by a servant. Elizabeth followed him into the room, with Miss Bingley at their heels.

"You two have killed her!" Miss Bingley suddenly accused.

"Whatever are you talking about?" Mr. Darcy asked.

"This slut is your mistress! Louisa must have discovered it, and so the two of you decided to silence her."

"What kind of nonsense are you spouting, Miss Bingley?" Mr. Darcy asked icily. "I demand that you apologise to Miss Bennet."

"I will not! I saw you come out from Miss Eliza's room. Your clothes are in disarray. Just look at yourselves! Her lips are swollen, and you have marks on your neck. She is your whore!"

"Dear heaven..." Mr. Bennet said from the open doorway. "Lizzy, is this...?"

Mr. Darcy interrupted him. "Mr. Bennet, your daughter has just done me the great honour of agreeing to become my wife."

"Engaged to Mr. Darcy! Ten thousand a year! The fine carriages! The pin money!" Mrs. Bennet squealed and rushed into the room to hug her daughter, and her wildly enthusiastic response effectively prevented her husband from demanding an immediate explanation from the young couple.

But Miss Bingley was another matter. Seeing her sister injured and her hope of becoming the Mistress of Pemberley dashed sent her into a fit. She shrieked, "No! No, I say! How can you possibly marry her! How could you choose her over me! She is nothing! She has no money, no connections, no style and no education!"

Mr. Bingley, who had just hurried in, said sharply, "Caroline, calm yourself and leave this room at once!" He came to the bedside and took Mrs. Hurst's limp hand in his own. "Darcy, what happened? Who did this to Louisa?"

But the mystery of Mrs. Hurst's injury was destined to go unsolved, for the victim never regained consciousness. Nevertheless, the unfortunate incident did not palpably hinder the ardent courtship and magnificent marriage of Mr. and Mrs. Darcy.

What if Mr. Darcy had a rakish soul?

RAKE DARCY

Mr. Fitzwilliam Darcy looked into the mirror and, startled, cried out, "Who are you?"

He turned to look at the man who stood a mere foot from him. How could it be possible? The man looked exactly like him, with just the same tall frame and dark, curly hair.

While he himself wore a black overcoat, matching waistcoat and breeches and a pristine white shirt, the man had everything in reverse. His coat, waistcoat and breeches were alabaster white, while his shirt was black. The other differences were that this stranger had olive skin and a reckless grin.

"I am your rakish soul," the man replied with a wink, and rubbed his hand over his thigh.

"Rakish soul? I do not believe it. You have the manner of an imposter."

"Do I not look exactly like you, Good Darcy?"

"My complexion is not so dark."

"Well, people normally associate rakish behaviour with the shadows. As your blackguard, I take on the darker complexion. But tell me, are not my eyes, nose, mouth and voice exactly like yours?"

Ignoring the question, Darcy said with conviction, "I do not have a rakish soul. I am an honourable man."

"Ah, but you are wrong. Every human is born evil. Only upbringing and education prevent them from staying evil. Still, I can reassure you, to a point. You were born with only a tiny bit of rakishness, not evil at all. You are mostly a good man, truth by told."

"You are a fake!" Darcy accused, but thoughts rose to assail him. *Am I turning mad? I am about to attend the Meryton Assembly. Should I instead stay in and send for a doctor for myself?*

"Do not be alarmed, Good Darcy. I appear here and now for a good reason."

"Why?"

"To show you how to court a lady." Rakish Darcy grinned. "And I shall be with you for a while. You may call me Rake Darcy."

"I do not intend to court any lady, and certainly not here in Hertfordshire. And you cannot make fun of my surname in this manner."

"Ah, but you cannot fight fate. I am part of you. Darcy is as much my surname as yours."

"Nonsense! I am devoted to caring for Georgiana until she has recovered from her heartache. Move aside," Darcy command. "And do not follow me."

"No one can see me, except you. And Georgiana needs a woman's hand. It will do her good when you find her a nice sister."

"You sounded like a match-making mama. Go away, charlatan!" With that, Darcy stalked out of the room. But when he glanced back, he saw his olive skin twin was following him, although Mr. Bingley, Mr. Hurst and the servants did not seem to notice the imposter.

Am I truly mad? he wondered.

"I say, Mr. Darcy, do you think we will be quite safe among the savages?" The angular voice of Miss Bingley woke him from his thought.

Darcy did not reply. He simply bowed to her. But his rakish soul walked near her, then pulled and clipped a long feather from her head. Her head jerked to the side and she cried out in pain. She did not seem to see Rake Darcy either. Darcy's mouth gaped open. He wanted to laugh but, as a true gentleman, he stifled the urge.

Bowing to Miss Bingley quickly again, he pulled her brother aside.

"Bingley, can we go in separate carriages?"

Bingley glanced at his sister, who was stomping her feet and swearing to herself, trying to tidy the unruly feathers. With a sigh, he nodded and asked Mr. Darcy to go ahead with his carriage, while he and the Hursts waited for Caroline. Miss Bingley tried to protest, but she was muffled by Rake Darcy.

Mr. Darcy turned a blind eye and settled into the carriage with trepidation. *Has my mind truly turned mad?*

"No, you are not mad. And Orange Lady's feathers are ugly!" Rake Darcy commented, appearing abruptly in front of him after the carriage had been on its way for several minutes.

Darcy's heart raced at the shock, but he folded his arms and said angrily, "She is my best friend's sister. You should not play tricks upon her."

"Bah! She is a bad influence! You will become a snobbish jerk if you continue to associate with her."

"No one can influence me. I am the master of my own self."

"Master, my ass! Once I have observed your behaviour tonight, I shall know how to label you."

Rake Darcy looked out of the window, exclaiming at the lovely scenery, the bright moon and the fresh air. He seemed as excited as a five-year-old boy on his first picnic.

Mr. Darcy gritted his teeth, refusing to talk to Rake. *I do not behave like this. He has no dignity or manners.*

When the carriage pulled up in front of the Assembly, Darcy panicked. He should have waited for Bingley. He did not know anyone else who would be attending, and he did not want to go into the hall alone. People would surely size him up, attempting to assess his wealth.

"Come on! We'll find lively music and merry ladies inside." Rake Darcy tugged him out of the carriage and pushed the reluctant Mr. Darcy, causing him to stagger forward.

The Assembly abruptly fell silent. Darcy halted in his tracks, flustered. He had never before stumbled into a gathering in such an inelegant manner.

An elderly gentleman came forward to greet him. "Sir William Lucas here. Welcome to our Assembly. I do not believe I have yet had the good fortune of making your acquaintance."

Mr. Darcy bowed with as much dignity as he could belatedly muster. "Fitzwilliam Darcy of Pemberley. I am a guest of Mr. Bingley. He has been delayed for a few moments."

"Capital! Capital! Mr. Bingley mentioned that you might be joining him."

While Sir William was asking him about his journey to Hertfordshire, Darcy caught sight of Rake Darcy skipping around the room, clipping more feathers from ladies' hats and then stopping in front of a group of three women.

Sir William followed the direction of Darcy's gaze and said jovially, "Oh, may I introduce you to Mrs. Bennet and her daughters?"

"Umh…" Darcy stammered as he saw Rake lowering his mouth to the earlobe of one of the younger ladies. She was extremely pretty, with blond hair, a serene countenance and a sweet smile. She did not seem to notice that she was mere inches away from being kissed.

Darcy gave his rakish soul a glare and walked toward the party quickly. *Stop, Rake! How could you do such a thing here?*

"…delighted to make your acquaintance." The sound of a high-pitched voice startled him, and he realized belatedly that Sir William had introduced him to the older lady.

Darcy could feel sweat beading on his brow. He had been so preoccupied by thinking how to stop Rake that he had ignored the women's greetings.

"Do you like to dance, Mr. Darcy?" Mrs. Bennet asked, looking annoyed. She tilted her head to the direction of the blond lady.

Seeing that Rake Darcy was circulating around that young woman, ogling her from every direction, Darcy closed his eyes for an instant and reasoned that a dance with the other maiden would at least allow him to draw his scoundrel twin away from the handsome woman who had captured the rogue's attention, if Rake was really here to observe him court a lady.

He turned to the younger lady and bowed. "Would you do me the honour of dancing with me?"

Mrs. Bennet frowned and murmured, "But surely you would like to dance with Jane first. She is prettier than Elizabeth..."

Darcy truly looked at Elizabeth Bennet for the first time. She was slightly shorter than Jane but she had a more womanly figure. While Jane had fair hair and angelic features, Elizabeth had dark curly hair and mischievous eyes. Although pretty in her own way, he supposed she was truly less traditionally handsome than Jane.

This will be a torture. She probably has no wit, Darcy thought glumly, and his jaw tightened.

However, seeing Rake Darcy's boorish behaviour toward Miss Jane, Darcy put out his hand decidedly.

At that, Elizabeth placed her hand on his and followed him out to the dance floor.

To his surprise, he felt a sudden thrill run through his body when she touched his hand. As they walked to the dance floor, he had to admit, at least, that she had good manners.

Uneasy with strangers, he remained silent. His gaze drifted off to search for his olive twin, wanting to know whether Rake had followed him to the dance floor.

"Do you regret your decision?"

The voice of his partner startled him. *At least she has a lively voice.* "What decision?" Darcy asked, and frowned, turning his attention more to his dance partner.

"Your decision to ask me to dance, instead of my sister."

"Why would you say that?"

"Your eyes seem to be turning more in her direction than concentrating on our dance."

"I only wanted to see whether my friend Mr. Bingley has arrived."

"I see you are not familiar with our neighbourhood. The entrance to the Assembly is that way, not where Jane is standing." She arched one brow, and her mouth curled up slightly on the right. *What a fine pair of eyes she has! Dark and sparkling when she flirts. And those lush cherry lips!* He drew in a deep breath. *She smells like fresh lavender, Mother's favourite fragrance.*

Rake Darcy's sneering voice startled him. "Caught on the spot, Good Darcy? It is an unforgivable offense to neglect your dance partner, especially one so lovely." The devilish man was standing right behind Elizabeth, mimicking her dance steps.

Darcy stared back at his rakish soul and bid Rake to desist with his eyes. His dance partner cocked her head and looked at him strangely. He bit his lip, reframed from bursting out with the scathing words he wanted to hurl at Rake.

Moving towards the end of the dancing line, Darcy's hands were touching Elizabeth's in one of the dance moves. Suddenly, Rake walked closer to her, wrapped his dark hands around her waist from behind, smoothed their way up the front of the dress, and cupped her gorgeous bosom.

Darcy stopped dead. His eyes nearly popped out. Such a magnificent pair of creamy mounds! His body boiled as he felt the sensation in his hands. *But how can this be? Rake caresses the lady, and I feel the tingle?*

Elizabeth stood still in front of him. She shivered, and her long eyelashes blinked quickly. Then she closed her eyes for a moment and leaned her head back toward Rake.

Darcy was outraged. He could not allow Rake to ravish Miss Elizabeth on the dance floor –

The music ended, and a sudden commotion startled him, and he looked to find that Bingley's party had finally arrived. A loud voice was speaking, and the people at the Assembly turned their attention to focus on their new neighbours.

Darcy seized the opportunity to pull Elizabeth out to the balcony.

Rake's devilish smile faded as he was separated from them. He called out after the pair, "I say, Good Darcy, where are you taking her? Don't be long. Her breasts are firm and bouncy. I want a good taste of them."

Upon hearing that outrageous demand, Darcy picked up his pace.

Once he had guided Elizabeth safely outside, the night air cooled his heated body. Under the bright light of a full moon, his gaze fell on his dance partner once again. Elizabeth's shimmering yellow gown seemed to glow, making her look like a golden goddess.

She was breathing heavily, her chest moving up and down. The cool air made her nipples stand up and push impudently against the thin muslin. Darcy suddenly had the urge to take his cue from Rake's words and suckle her hard. But he called upon his self-control and resisted those thoughts.

"What happened?" she whispered, and the husky timbre of her voice helped to distract him from his ungentlemanly thoughts.

Darcy nervously brushed at his hair with an unsteady hand and turned to look up at the sky. "It is too hot inside."

"You do not want to greet your friends?"

"Miss Binlgey is not my favourite person." After the words came out, he clamped his mouth shut. *It is Rake! He is a bad influence.*

"She intends to snare you?"

"How did you know?"

"You immediately escaped out here when I heard her ask where you were."

"Did she indeed?"

She nodded. "Rather loudly."

"It is unfortunate that Bingley has such a sister." *What has happened to my discretion? I am confiding unkind opinions about Miss Bingley to a total stranger!*

"I have three rather silly younger sisters, myself. We cannot choose our relations. What about you?"

Darcy's countenance turned grave. "I have a younger sister, twelve years my junior. Georgiana used to be cheery and lively, but a…misadventure, this past summer, has changed her." *Why am I confiding in her, rather than Bingley? Perhaps the appearance of Rake Darcy has shaken me up.*

"I am sorry to hear of it. Did you not want her to be here with you?" she asked softly.

Her compassionate expression urged him on. "I blame myself for her misadventure. My aunt and uncle thought my self-berating mood was disruptive to Georgiana's recovery. So they took her in, for the time being, and urged me to travel here to visit Mr. Bingley."

"And you miss her."

He nodded. "Our mother died when Georgiana was but two. I love my sister dearly."

"And your father?"

"He died five years ago."

"You miss your father's guidance and your mother's gentleness."

He nodded again. *How can she understand so much about me?*

"You have soulful eyes. I can see that your parents were very dear to you and still mean a great deal to you, even now."

Looking straight into her tender gaze, Darcy suddenly felt a sense of belonging. It was like coming home, where he could share life's ups and downs with someone who truly understood him, even without words.

His defenses fell away, and he began to pour out the sense of disappointment, anger and betrayal that he felt towards his childhood friend, George Wickham, although he was still cautious enough not to disclose Georgiana's failed elopement.

"I sometimes think that all of humanity is born evil." Elizabeth touched his hand to comfort him. "Only good breeding and education prevent them from staying evil. It is tragic that Mr. Wickham did not take advantage of the excellent opportunity with which your family provided him."

She is saying exactly the same thing as Rake! How can that be?

She turned her face to the sky and said, in a more cheerful tone, "But then I remember our Lord. He provides us with guidance and good examples. I am happy to say that I know more good people than bad...but you must take into account that I only dine with four-and-twenty families regularly."

Darcy smiled at her jest. *Do I know more virtuous souls than vile ones? Indeed I do. Will I be able to forgive Wickham? Perhaps...one day.*

In the meantime, here stood a beautiful lady with sense and sensitivity, watching him with glittering eyes. She was altogether worthy of his attention. Gently, he brushed a wayward curl behind her ear and whispered, "Miss Elizabeth Bennet, would you do me the honour of dancing with me again?"

"Another dance? Are you sure that you are up to such an undertaking?" She arched her brows but did not take his hand.

He nodded. "I believe so. I know, now, that you have three silly sisters."

"And a match-making mother," she added, and smiled.

"Well, I meet many of those in London society." He returned her smile.

"My aunt and uncle live in Cheapside," she cautioned, but she put her hand in his.

"The late great-grandfather of Mr. Bingley lived not far from there, as well." He squeezed her soft hand and placed it on the crook of his arm.

In accord, they walked back into the hall, chatting eagerly.

That night, although the good people of Hertfordshire did not know enough to recognize the rarity, they were treated to the genuine smile and laugh of Mr. Fitzwilliam Darcy.

Miss Bingley nearly fainted upon seeing him escort Elizabeth Bennet to the floor for the third set of dances.

As for Rake Darcy, luckily for all concerned, he did not make a further appearance that night.

What if Netherfield Park was haunted?

WHEN THE DEAD INTERFERE

"My dear Mr. Bennet," said his lady to him one day, "have you heard that Netherfield Park is let at last?"

"But, Mama," exclaimed Lydia, their youngest daughter, "that house is haunted! Who can have been so droll as to let it?"

Mrs. Bennet snorted. "Nonsense. Your uncle Philips assures Mr. Bingley, who is a young man of large fortune from the north, that the house is in superb order..."

***

Soon, the Bingleys moved in and became acquainted with the Bennets, who were but three miles away. Jane Bennet, the eldest daughter, visited the Bingley sisters one day, but became sick after being caught in the rain. Our story continues as in the original tale until the last night of Jane and Elizabeth's stay at Netherfield. It was not until the last day of October that the boundary between the living and the deceased dissolved.

***

"I am quite bored with this visit!" The elegant elderly lady stretched her arms above her head and danced a little step away from her companion.

"Emma, that is a most unladylike gesture! We need to uphold our manner, even in the land of darkness," the handsome old man chided.

Pouting, Emma folded her arms across her bosom. "Oh, Mr. Knightley, you are such a bore! I do not understand why I agreed to marry you at all, when we were alive. And I especially do not understand why we are still together now that we are dead."

Knightley came to her and wrapped his arms around her slim waist. With a serious countenance, he said, "Just think what sort of havoc my little Emma would create in the world, if not for my constant vigilance. I cannot leave you, my dear, day or night." He then lowered his head to give her a quick kiss on the lips.

Emma unfolded her arms and pushed him away. "George, we only have a few hours to play with the living. Let us not waste time. You can kiss me any other day of the year. We will be going back to Hartfield soon." She then ran upstairs, as quickly as her elderly legs could manage, happily.

Knightley chased after her. "Now, Emma, what do you have in mind? I do not want you to scare any of the young people to death. I heard that it has been many years since Netherfield had a family living here."

She went through the door of the first bedchamber. When he caught up with her in the room, they could see a plain-looking man lying on the bed, snoring loudly.

Emma held her nose with her fingers and frowned. "He stinks! I wager he drank more than three glasses of brandy, and whatever else was on offer tonight."

"Let us leave him alone then. You do not want to play with a drunkard."

"What do you say we make him want never to drink again? You can turn into a big barrel of foul-tasting wine and press onto him heavily, giving him nightmares. I wager he would not go near a drink anymore, after such an experience," she said with a mischievous grin.

"Emma! And here I thought you only liked to play at matchmaking!" He tried to pull her away from the bed.

"I know, but he is already married to this Lousia, so I cannot make a match for him."

"How do you know about that?" he asked.

"I like to listen in on the lives of the living, from time to time. Mr. Hurst likes to drink and sleep. His wife is called Lousia. They seldom spend their nights together. In fact, they have not done so once since they moved to Netherfield. But you are right, my dear. Matchmaking is my favourite. I know what I shall do." With a quick turn, she disappeared, leaving nothing but a puff of white.

Luckily, he could find her anywhere. With a fast swirl of the air and another puff of white, he joined her in another bedroom, where she was perched on a chair beside a bed where a handsome young man lay sleeping.

"George, young Darcy here loves the lively lady staying in the guest chamber, Miss Elizabeth Bennet. Unfortunately, he has the laughable notion that, since she has no connections or money, and has a mother and sisters who are improper, he should not show her any sign of admiration. Shall I make him confess to her?"

"How can you do that? We do not possess the magical power to make the living speak as we want!" Knightley rolled his eyes and shook his head. After so many years of marriage, he still did not understand how his wife could unerringly find all the gossip of the world.

"All things are possible. I can put him and Miss Elizabeth in the same room, and I can turn quite scary every time he does not reveal his true feelings to her. Let me wake him and take him to his heart's desire."

Knightley put his hand on her arm. "Wait, Emma. You might well scare them both to death."

"Well then, if you do not like that plan, I suppose I could strike him on the head every time he does the wrong thing."

"You will knock him witless then. Do you want to do that to a sensible young man?"

"What *would* you have me do, then? It is only on this night that I can play at matchmaking for the living," Emma said, pouting again. But then her face brightened. "I know! I shall simply put him in her bed. I know how much he loves to gaze upon the form of the fair maiden. He will not be able to resist her, when he lies so close beside her. He will simply *have* to marry her, after tonight!" She clapped her hands, congratulating herself on the brilliant idea.

"How do you know that the young man lusts after this Elizabeth? Did you see more than you should?" It was his turn to fold his arms across his chest, as he was seriously displeased at the idea of his wife looking at another man.

"You know I cannot 'peek' into the goings-on of the living when we were in our world. But I listened. He talked in his sleep from time to time; and then I even heard him providing his own relief, once or twice, and crying out Elizabeth's name in his moment of ecstasy."

"Emma, you are shameless!"

"I am an old, married woman with several children. I know all about men and their needs."

"Still! To eavesdrop on a single young man of the living world! It is not the right way to interfere. Do you even know whether the young lady likes him or not? If she does not, you will only create a forced marriage, one for which Miss Bennet certainly will not thank you. Let us leave the living to their lives. We should take a stroll in the moonlight. We have not done that for a long time." Knightley then pulled her hand to the crook of his arm and took her away from Darcy's room.

Unknown to the good couple, Frank Churchill had been listening to their conversation. Much like Emma, he also liked to play with the living, but he liked perverse jokes better, and so he decided to do precisely what Knightley had opposed: he lifted Darcy's sleeping body and transported him to Miss Elizabeth's room.

How did he know where Miss Elizabeth slept? He eavesdropped on the living, of course, just as Emma liked to do. Life in the dark was boring. He had thought for a moment about whether to deliver this Darcy to Miss Bingley or Mrs. Hurst, but he did not think it would work. The young man would not be aroused by them. He had also considered taking Mr. Darcy to the other Miss Jane Bennet, but reasoned that she might still be too weak to entertain him.

By the time Churchill put Mr. Darcy down to lie besides Miss Elizabeth, he was out of breath. He hated this weakly ghost form of himself. He was no longer a handsome man, and his hair was almost gone. His body was so big that he could hardly see his shoes, and his face was covered with wrinkles. Worst of all, he was no longer aroused by fair maidens, and could no longer accomplish the manly act. Otherwise, he would have loved to trifle with many of the fair maidens who had lived in Netherfield in years past.

Churchill took a look at Miss Elizabeth. *She is not as pretty as my Jane was when she was in her bloom. But this gentlewoman has quick wit and a temper. She should be a passionate thing in bed. And I heard her protesting to her sister that she did not like this young man at all. It will be fun to see her response when she awakens to find him in her bed. Ah, but I had best tie her up, or she will scratch his eyes out before he can trifle with her. I shall stick the locks of the main and servant doors, and then she will be unable to escape him!* He laughed at his own scheme.

Churchill duly tied the wrists and ankles of the lady to the bedposts, then knocked both Darcy and Elizabeth on the head slightly, and sat back on a chair, intending to watch…

"Frank, where are you?"

The scream of his wife gave him shivers. The pretty, compliant Jane Fairfax he had married so many years ago had turned into a shrew not long after she gave birth to their first daughter. She never recovered her light and pleasing form; worse yet, she started to indulge in drinking. She grew as ugly as a pig, and soon started hitting him when she was drunk. He never thought he would be rendered witless by a mere woman.

"Where are you, old man? I shall skin you alive when I find you!" Her voice was nearer, and he swore at his damn luck. He had hoped to enjoy watching a bit of passionate mating, but now, instead, he had to run. *Why can she not leave me alone on this one day of merriment?* He stood up immediately and, with a twist of his body and a puff of white, left Elizabeth's room in great haste.

***

Mr. Darcy felt a slight pain in the back of his head and woke up. Bright moonlight shone onto the bed. *This is not my bed chamber in Netherfield*, he realized with a shock. The room was similar, but the hangings were in pink, rather than dark brown, And the curtains and furniture were more suited to the tastes of a –

He felt the warmth of a body beside him, and heard a soft moan. He turned around on the bed and, with the help of the moon's light, saw that it was Miss Elizabeth

Bennet lying there. Her eyes were half closed, and she was moving slightly, as if she were about to wake up.

He sucked in a quick breath. *What is she doing here? Does she intend to use her arts and allurements to make me forget what I owe to myself and to all my family? How dare she? I thought she was different from the fawning women of the ton. Indeed, I had imagined her to be superior to the likes of Miss Bingley!*

A sudden anger surged in his chest. He stripped the bed sheet off her body, intending to send her away immediately...

Darcy's eyes widened when he saw that she was bound to the bed. Her hands were tied to the bedpost, high above her head, and her legs were pulled apart and bound, as well.

Did I do that? Did I come here to her room and tie her up? Is this a dream?

Mr. Darcy focused on Elizabeth's tempting form. He had wanted to admire her figure for many days. She looked very real. Her feet were so small, he could palm them easily. As the hem of her night dress was hiked up, he could see the skin of her legs. They looked as smooth as those of a newborn. Under the thin layer of cloth, he continued his survey. He swallowed hard upon seeing her supple thighs, wide hips and narrow waist. Then his gaze reached her bosom. The creamy globes were hardly contained by the thin green nightgown. They were rising and falling rapidly, dangerously close to pushing the nipples out from their confinement with each upward movement.

Darcy's arousal came on with full force upon seeing such a lovely vision. He licked his lips. *What a dream! I do not want to wake up!* He decided to take advantage of it before the tempting vision of Miss Elizabeth disappeared. Lowering his mouth, he pressed a wet kiss to her cleavage. *She smells wonderful! A mixture of rose, lavender and maiden sweat!* With her hands bound above her, he could not pull the straps of her night dress down her shoulders, and so he set himself to unfastening the tiny buttons that ran down the front of her gown instead. When he had freed a dozen of them, he folded back the halves of the fabric bodice and feasted his eyes on the result. Indeed, he felt like a hungry infant who could not get enough of her. His tongue traced the gorgeous fullness of her breasts with a connoisseur's reverence. *What a vision! Finally, I can devour her as I like.*

He was about to lower his head to suckle her rosy nipples when the shaking, tentative voice of Elizabeth made him raise his head. "What... are you doing here?" He could see that she was wide awake now. She wore a touchingly vulnerable look, and she pulled at the cloths that bound her hands and legs. When she was not successful at freeing herself, she demanded more forcefully, "Mr. Darcy, what are you doing to me?"

He trailed his fingers from her brow, down her cheek to her lips, and replied, "I like this dream. We can still duel verbally, but you can no longer misunderstand my meaning. I am mad for you, and I intend to ravish you now."

Her eyes widened with fright. "A dream? Are you not a gentleman? How can you ravish a maiden, even in a dream?"

He laughed out loud, which made him look young and carefree. "I have often dreamed of making love to you before, teaching you the pleasures of man and woman. In my mind, you were always hesitant but responsive. I have had much pleasure from you. But I never before dreamed of ravishing you with your hands bound. I'll wager that my gentlemanly nature has lessened under the pressure of your tempting allurements over these past few days." He grazed his cheek on her breasts roughly, then slipped his hands under her nightdress and gently squeezed her inner thighs, pretending to be a rogue.

She felt less frightened, reassured by his smile, half-convinced that it was indeed a dream. But his manly ministrations made her heart jump. Something not right. "You dreamt of making me yours? I do not believe it! You said I was not handsome enough to tempt you! You must be just a scoundrel who takes pleasure in trifling with gentlewomen."

Mr. Darcy lowered his mouth and nibbled her upper lip until she was left breathless. "I apologize," he murmured at last. "I had not the heart to socialise when I first arrived in Hertfordshire. My sister had not yet fully recovered from a disheartening experience during the summer. I was preoccupied and worried about her. But I had not had the heart to refuse Bingley's invitation either, as he has been such a good friend to me. I had not even looked at you properly when I said those words. Not long thereafter, I realised that I found your form light and pleasing, your wit challenging, and your attitude altogether refreshing." He rubbed his body against her side and said, "You see? I am all hot and hard now. I find you more than tempting. And I am no scoundrel. I have not trifled with any maiden before. I swear. You were my wife when you laid with me in the dreams."

He saw her face turn bright red, and her breathing became shallow. "Your wife? Then your intentions are honourable? You do not look down upon the society of Meryton? The reason you did not speak to us was not because you considered us confined and unvarying?"

He pressed his fingertips against her neck, feeling the fast pulsation of her blood. Then he lowered his hands to cup her breasts, and watched with satisfaction while her expression grew dazed as he squeezed and kneaded the creamy twin peaks. He did not feel called upon to explain himself. This was a dream, was it not? He would much rather enjoy her heavenly body. However, ever the true gentleman, he replied, "Pemberley is situated in the country, too. I love the country better than town. I am just not very good at conversing with strangers." He then remembered her words of the other day. His hands stopped and he asked uncertainly, "Do you indeed find me vain and prideful?"

She could hardly gather her wits. Suppressing a moan at the cessation of his caresses, she said, "You slighted me at our first meeting. You did not talk to people at our gatherings. I fear I drew an unfortunate conclusion."

But her tactful wording did not suffice. Mr. Darcy was so disappointed that he stopped his ministrations, and drew the unbuttoned halves of her bodice together to cover her bosom. Then he sat up and, with difficulty, untied her. "I thought you welcomed me. You defended me to your mother. You challenged my thinking at every turn. I thought that was your way to make me aware of you and flirt with me. You attracted me more than I liked. I even decided that no sign of admiration should escape me, nothing that could elevate you with the hope of influencing my felicity. How very wrong I am!"

· Freed, Elizabeth sat up as well. She pulled the bed sheet up to cover herself. "I am truly confused. You did not want me to have hope in you, and yet in your dream, you made me your wife."

Mr. Darcy stood up and paced the room, then stopped suddenly before her and, without warning, poured his heart out. "What could I do? In vain I have struggled. My feelings will not be repressed. I admire and love you ardently. But could you expect me to rejoice in the inferiority of your connections? To congratulate myself on the hope of relations, whose condition in life is so decidedly beneath my own? And the situation of your mother's family, though objectionable, is nothing in comparison to that total want of propriety so frequently, so almost uniformly betrayed by herself and by your three younger sisters."

Stung, Elizabeth stood up, hands on her hips, and replied, "I find your address both offending and insulting. I have never desired your good opinion, and you have certainly bestowed it most unwillingly. From the very beginning, from the first moment, I may almost say, of my acquaintance with you, your manners, impressing me with the fullest belief of your ..."

"Stop!" The sudden sound of an elderly woman's voice made Mr. Darcy and Elizabeth whirl around in surprise. They stiffened at the sight of an elderly couple sitting on the bed they had so recently vacated.

"Who are you?" Mr. Darcy said.

"What are you doing here?" Elizabeth asked.

"I am Mrs. Emma Knightley, and this is my husband, George." The elderly woman turned slightly as she introduced the elderly man. When her body moved, the moonlight seemed to dim. Mr. Darcy and Elizabeth's eyes widened on seeing that the bodies of their strange visitors were almost transparent. Indeed, they could see through the elderly couple to the other side of the room.

Elizabeth gasped, then threw herself against Mr. Darcy. Wrapping her arms around his neck, she cried out in alarm, "Is this still a dream? Are they ghosts?"

"I warned you, Emma, that you would scare them to death!" Mr. Knightley said.

"Do not be afraid, Miss Elizabeth. We are good ghosts, and this is not a dream. It is Samhain*, the time when we can appear in the living world. I know that Mr. Darcy truly loves you. I only wanted him to admit to wanting you as his wife, and to see the two of you happily together."

Mr. Darcy was shaken, as well. He wrapped his arms protectively around Elizabeth and pulled her as tightly against him as possible. But, as a man, he vowed to be brave. "Mrs. Knightley," he said, firmly addressing the lady ghost, "I do not appreciate your interference. I am an adult, and I know what is best for myself. As it happens, your actions did not help. Miss Bennet found my admiration...wanting."

"Bah! She found your *address* wanting. Young man, you cannot tell a woman that you love her, in one breath, and then insult her family, in another next. You will be marrying her, not her family. Your aunt Lady Catherine de Bourgh is as objectionable, in her way, as any of the Bennet ladies. You should be ashamed of yourself. And did you think clearly about your own character? Your ten thousand a year cannot tempt this girl to marry you. You will need to mend your arrogant ways and truly cherish her. Now, take this frightened young girl to bed and do your manly best to please her."

"Emma!" Mr. Knightley chastised his wife.

"What? This young man has certainly thought about ravishing her often enough. Why should I pretend that he has had no such thoughts, now that Miss Bennet is in his arms and the doors cannot be opened?"

At that, Mr. Darcy released Elizabeth just long enough to check on the door to the corridor. The lock was twisted, as if it had been smashed by a hammer. He pulled at it a few times, but it would not move at all. He then walked to the door that opened to the servants' entrance. It was in a similar state.

"What kind of ghosts are you? You brought me here, bound Miss Bennet, and made the locks unworkable, all in the name of matchmaking. Have you no shame? I demand that you fix the doors immediately."

Mr. Knightley defended his wife, "Emma did not transport you here, nor did we bind Miss Elizabeth or damage the locks. It was all Churchill's doing. He is a spineless ghost who enjoys playing twisted jokes on the living. And, although I am sorry to disappoint you, we do not possess the magical power to undo what he has done."

Elizabeth gasped in distress. "Oh, please! You can pass through walls. Can you not take Mr. Darcy to his bedroom that way? He cannot be found in here in the morning!" she pleaded.

"We are ghosts, and so we can indeed go through walls. But Mr. Darcy is alive. He cannot. Do you want me to kill him and shove his body out of the window, all so that your reputation can remain unsullied?" Emma asked, baring her teeth.

"No!" cried Elizabeth and Knightley together.

Elizabeth ran back to Darcy and held onto him tightly. "Mr. Darcy is a good brother and a good friend. And he has many tenants who depend upon him. I would not have such a man harmed simply to protect my reputation." Elizabeth said indignantly from within the sheltering curve of his arm.

Emma adopted a menacing countenance. "But you do not like him. He has seen you in almost your full glory. How can you marry another? Is it not better that he be dead?"

"No," Elizabeth objected staunchly. "I was only prejudiced against him in the past, disappointed that such a handsome and eligible man found me lacking. Now that I know his true feelings, if he can bear with my family, I would be most happy to accept him."

Emma clapped her hands. "Excellent! And what do you say, young man?"

Mr. Darcy held tight to Elizabeth, also fearing for his life, as there was no telling how a ghost might act. "Elizabeth, I apologize for looking down on your relations. I would be most honoured if you would consent to be my wife."

She nodded and whispered, "It will be my honour!"

"Marvelous!" Emma cheered. "Now, young man, take her to bed and start making babes. I promise that we will not peek. I shall even keep Jane and Frank Churchill away. But I will not leave entirely until I hear her maidenly cries of ecstasy," Emma declared, then disappeared in a puff of white.

Mr. Darcy and Elizabeth turned bright red.

Mr. Knightley cleared his throat. "I am sorry, Mr. Darcy and Miss Bennet. You need not do as Emma said. I shall try to keep her out of here. Either way, it is almost dawn. She and I will need to return to the land of darkness soon." With that, Mr. Knightley bowed and disappeared, as well.

At that, Elizabeth fainted. Had she not swooned and required his strong arms, Mr. Darcy thought that he himself might well have fainted from fear, as well.

Rallying, he swept her up in his arms and placed her on the bed. Going to the wash stand, he dampened a cloth, then returned to the bedside to press it to her forehead and throat, his hands shaking.

Words rose, unbidden, to his lips and spilled forth, baring his deepest thoughts and feelings. "Elizabeth, I love you. Please do not fall ill from the shock of this night. I shall truly honour my promise to marry and cherish you. I shall learn to bear with your relations. Mrs. Knightley, though overbearing, was right. I have been a selfish being, all my life. As a child, I was taught to care for none beyond my own family circle, and to think lowly of all the rest of the world. Such I was, from eight to eight-and-twenty; and such I might still be but for you, dearest, loveliest Elizabeth! What do I not owe you! You have taught me a lesson, one that was hard indeed, at first, but one that is most advantageous. Please wake up, Elizabeth, and say again that you will be mine."

Elizabeth's eyes slowly opened. She had heard his entire whole-hearted declaration, and she now reached up to caress his face with the gentlest of hands.

"Mr. Darcy, you must forgive me, as well. I was blinded by prejudice about your character and behaviour only because you slighted me. I took every chance I could to challenge you, in an attempt to show you that I was superior to the elegant ladies you had known. I was vain and prideful, as well. I did not know my own mind. I feel honoured and gratified that you love me…but I will not hold you to your promise. After all, it was only made under threat from the ghosts."

Mr. Darcy held her face and spoke with passionate regard. "Not so. My wishes and affection are unchanged. Elizabeth, marry me!"

She returned his gaze and replied, in a firm, clear voice, "It is my honour, Mr. Darcy."

He lowered his head and gave her a passionate kiss…which led to another. And another. What better way was there to drive away fear with this, the most pleasant of pursuits? It was not long before Mr. Darcy was lying half atop of Elizabeth's body, stroking her breast through the thin fabric of her night dress. He stopped and was about to steel himself to move away when she said, "Make me yours, Mr. Darcy! Please, teach me the pleasure of man and woman, just as in your dreams."

"Are you certain that this is what you want, my love? Are you sure that you are not still frightened by the threat from Mrs. Knightley?"

Elizabeth sat up and shook her head. "I was actually…quite disappointed just now, when you stopped touching me." Then she buried her head against his shoulder and murmured. "You must be disgusted by me. Such wanton behaviour! I declare, I am no better than Lydia!"

Mr. Darcy eased her back onto the bed and cupped her face again. "Ah, but there is no shame in wanting your beloved. In fact, it will make our marriage bed most enjoyable. But your father may demand a long engagement. I would not want to have to confess to him that I had taken your virtue, or that we are forced to marry immediately because I have gotten you with child."

"Oh!" Elizabeth said, clearly disappointed.

He chuckled. "But I know of many ways to teach you about the pleasures of the flesh without endangering your virtue. Do you trust me?"

She nodded enthusiastically. Darcy smiled, and slowly removed her night dress. When she lay naked in front of his eyes, he was gobsmacked. She was beautiful, her manner shy and yet eager. He bestowed kisses upon her face, lips, shoulders, breasts, nipples, abdomen and down to her apex.

When he parted her legs and licked her wet womanhood, she squirmed and moaned aloud, letting him know the pleasure he was giving her, encouraging him to do more. He tasted her folds and pressed his tongue into her entrance, in and out, mimicking the mating action, while his hands continued to cup and stroke her bosom.

Elizabeth was overwhelmed. His hands and lips were like magic. She cried out loudly as she reached her climax. Her inner muscles convulsed and contracted, and she screamed in astonished delight, for the sensation was utterly unknown to her.

When she finally stopped shivering and trembling, he lay by her side to catch his breath. Her peak had shaken his control; indeed, he had nearly come when her leg accidentally brushed against his shaft.

As her wits returned, she asked, "May I... return the favour, my dear?" Her eyes sparkled with curiosity.

"Are you certain?"

"I am certain of nothing, unschooled as I am in these arts, and yet I hope that you will find me a most eager and determined pupil."

Ecstatic that she was proving to be so brave a woman, Mr. Darcy asked her permission to take off his night clothes. Although she averted her glance, she did not shy away when he did so and then pulled her on top on him. He stroked the curve of her pert bottom and moved her body up and down to tease his manhood. When her wet folds rubbed against him, his arousal, which had already been substantial, sprang even to attention. His breath caught, and he devoted himself to kissing her mouth and playing with her gorgeous breasts.

Elizabeth, emboldened, soon braced her hands on his chest and rode him as she would have ridden a horse astride. Although he was not inside of her, she was excited by each contact with his velvety hard shaft, which pulsed and shook like a wayward and excited animal.

Experiencing these ministrations, Darcy could not long bear to lie passively. Of a sudden, he turned her over and straddled her. Encouraging her to wrap her legs around his waist, he played the head of his proud rod along her drenched womanhood, nearly maddened by the need not to claim her fully. He suckled her nipples in such a mad frenzy that it brought her to another climax. Instinctively, she tightened her legs around him, raising her body from the bed and twisting against him intimately.

Unprepared for her wild action, Darcy reached his peak almost immediately. Wrenching aside, he gritted his teeth to stop the loud groan of satisfaction as his seed spilled onto the bed sheet. Then he collapsed on top of her.

When the sun finally rose above the horizon, the ghosts returned to their world. While Elizabeth called for help to smash open the doors to her bed chamber, Mr.

Darcy hid in the dressing room, and later returned to his room with no one the wiser concerning his nocturnal adventures.

But when he and Mr. Bingley accompanied the Miss Bennets back to Longbourn, he lost no time in asking for permission to marry Miss Elizabeth.

They were wed two months later, in a double ceremony with Bingley and Jane. During the weeks of their engagement, Mr. Darcy and Elizabeth grew to know each other much better, and found that they were fine complements to each other, both in temperament and in their views about the world.

There was, however, a sad incident that resulted from Bingley's stay at Netherfield. It seemed that Miss Bingley had witnessed two ugly, elderly ghosts named Jane and Frank Churchill in a brawl in her bed chamber during the last night of October. She was frightened nearly to death, and fled to seek her sister Louisa's help. After that, she refused to sleep alone, demanding that Louisa stay by her side. Bingley cancelled the lease on Netherfield after his marriage and moved to an estate in Derbyshire, while Miss Bingley lived with her sister ever after.

As for Emma Knightley, although she did not cause Miss Bingley's fright, she received a thorough chiding from her husband. Mr. Knightley took her back to Hartfield, while Jane and Frank Churchill continued to haunt Netherfield Park.

A few years later, Mr. Darcy and Elizabeth named their second daughter Emma, in honour of the overbearing ghost who had so successfully brought along their earlier understanding.

* Samhain, a festival in Celtic cultures, has some elements of a festival of the dead.

FANTASY

What if Mr. Darcy was a warlord?

LEATHER KILT AND RED COAT

Once upon a time, in the deep southern world, there was a kingdom called Austenland. War was raging, and men were scarce there.

After all of the servants had been recruited, the militia was asked to search every house for men, young or old, gentlemen or not, to serve the country. It was rumoured that the army would descend upon Meryton the next day, by dawn.

Mrs. Bennet heard the news and went into hysterics.

"Mr. Bennet! Mr. Bennet! What can we do? We have no son but five daughters. What if the red coats take you away? You might be killed, as you are old and weak. Then we will certainly be thrown out of Longbourn by that hateful Mr. Collins. Oh, my nerves!"

"Ah, but my dear, Mr. Collins will have been taken away by the militia already, being the last man in Rosings and Hunsford," Mr. Bennet replied calmly.

"In times of great turmoil, we should all join our hands and strive for the greater glory of Austenland. Papa, I urge you to volunteer your service," Mary declared.

"Papa, perhaps you can talk some sense into the enemy when you meet them. Surely there is no need for fighting. and not every one can be that bad," Jane murmured.

Coughing, Kitty added timidly, "I would not mind meeting some red coats."

"La, I love red coats!" Lydia, the youngest daughter, jumped into the conversation. "I would love being handled by a camp full of soldiers."

"Lizzy, you are very quiet. What silly idea do you have, in addition to those of your sisters?" Mr. Bennet asked.

"I think all of them seem to make sense." Elizabeth said.

"What? Are you out of your mind?" Mr. Bennet could not believe that his clever, favourite child could entertain such an idea.

"I say that we should hide you when the militia comes, and that I shall disguise myself as a man and go in your place," she announced with a determined glint in her eye.

"I thought of the idea first," Lydia exclaimed. "Let me go!"

"No, Lydia. Let Lizzy go." Mrs. Bennet took a protesting Lydia to one side, for Lydia was her favourite, and she did not want her to be sacrificed for her elderly father. She whispered to her, "Did you not hear that the enemy tortures and kills the members of our army? Your Aunt Philips said that the River Thames has turned pink from the blood of our men, and that Hoyden Park was covered with the remains of red coats."

"But she does not live near the River Thames or Hoyden Park. How can she be certain?" Lydia argued. "I want to be in a camp full of soldiers!"

"I shall make you some red coats with old muslin and ribbon," Mrs. Bennet said. "I am sure that, in no time, the war will end and men will return to court you. You are the tallest and have the liveliest disposition."

The compliments seemed to do the trick, soothing Lydia's ego. With a pout, she agreed and walked away.

When the sun rose the next day, several officers came to Longbourn. Before they could search the house, Elizabeth, dressed in gentleman's clothes, volunteered to go with them. The officers were happy to be met with such co-operation, and they did not bother to search for other men at Longbourn.

Elizabeth thought she would be assigned to do some manual job befitting a fit young "man" from the countryside. Instead, she was given several tests, upon arriving at the camp near Londonland, and was ranked as a Colonel and sent to work as General Darcy's assistant.

Before she entered the great man's office, she heard a deep voice saying, "This Bennet scored well in the test. But are you sure he is not a fake? I cannot believe that a savage neighbourhood like Meryton can produce a person with such fine qualities and intelligence."

Elizabeth saw red. She had no interest in serving this arrogant man. She decided that she would taunt him whenever she could, hoping for a transfer soon.

When she entered the room, she was shocked by the sight. General Darcy was alone, except for a tiny grey kangaroo with a smiling face. Who had he been talking to?

Most militia wore a red coat, buttoned up from head to toe, like she herself. But General Darcy wore something altogether different. Indeed, he did not wear anything at all except a short leather kilt and a pair of long leather boots. He was exceptionally tall, perhaps six foot five. His shoulders were broad and his chest muscles looked hard.

Elizabeth had a great urge to put her pale hands against his browned chest, just to see the contrast.

"Welcome, Bennet." A friendly sound woke her from her revel. The kangaroo had spoken!

"Bingley at your service." He bounced towards her and extended his paw. "I am General Darcy's advisor."

Darcy snorted. "He is my sister's pet. Now stop staring at my body and sit down. I want to test you myself."

When he turned to walk to his desk, Elizabeth's gaze followed the swaying of the leather kilt, and the sight of his hairy legs. She gulped for air and followed him immediately. All thought of demanding a transfer seemed to have drained out of her head.

Darcy opened the cabinet behind him and took out a bottle of red wine. He poured one glass for Elizabeth and one for himself.

"Drink up!" he commanded.

Elizabeth held his gaze and drank it.

He gulped down his wine and scowled at her. "Too slow." He poured another glass for each of them.

She did as she was told and swallowed the second glass more quickly. Not a word was spoken between them; the only communication was their hot stares, as four bottles were consumed.

"See? I told you Bennet was good." Bingley laughed. "I will leave you two." He bounced out of the room and closed the door.

"You are ...not bad," Darcy said as he stood up unsteadily to clap Elizabeth on the shoulder. The move overbalanced them both, and they ended up crashing down onto the floor, with her pinned under him. Both immediately fell into a drunken sleep.

In the morning, Darcy began by testing her skill at throwing darts. From there, the tests went on for several days. But Darcy woke up each morning with the strange feeling that he had been caressed and fondled in his dreams. He also seemed to remember breathing in the most alluring lavender scent during the whole night. Every morning, he found his body throbbing with...needs. But Bennet was a man, so Darcy was puzzled to realize that he had repeatedly experienced dreams of being with a woman.

He decided to get to the bottom of the matter; today he would not conduct the test himself. He asked Bingley to drink, toast for toast, with Bennet, and he observed them both while standing aside. He could see that the young soldier seemed very nervous, his gaze darting to Darcy from time to time.

Bennet was drunk by the sixth bottle. Darcy shooed Bingley out of his office, picked Bennet up and walked through the door to his sleeping quarters. When he placed him on the bed, Bennet suddenly spoke in a woman voice.

"Arrogant pig, I hate you," the sleepy soldier murmured. "But you have the most virile body. Your chest hair tastes delicious, and I love to twirl my finger around your cute navel..."

Darcy's eyes widened. A woman in disguise? So that was what had been happening every morning before he awoke. He could not believe that the recruitment officers had failed to discover her true identity before sending her to his office.

Telling himself that it was his duty to verify the truth, he unbuttoned Bennet's uniform jacket.

Ah, such creamy alabaster skin! But her bosom was bound flat. What a pity!

His arousal came on, full force. He was tempted to strip her bare and bury himself deep inside her. But General

Darcy did not force himself on any woman, particularly not on one who was largely unconscious. Nevertheless, he could not bring himself to simply walk away.

Rising, he locked the door, then stripped off his clothes and stretched out beside her.

The sun shone inside the bedchamber, and Elizabeth woke to the musky smell of the General. She smiled, remembering her daring actions the past few mornings, when Darcy had yet to awaken. She had kissed nearly every inch of his body, except those forbidden parts hidden beneath his leather kilt. After all, she was a maiden. The man did not have a clue about her fondling him...

She blinked her eyes, remembering the heavy drinking of the previous night. And when she tried to raise her body, she noticed that she was pinned down by a strong body.

She opened her eyes more widely, and saw General Darcy's bright smile. His angular body was heavy on top of her. She drew in a deep breath, and was alarmed to realize that she was nude, as was he.

"What are you doing?" she said. She could not help but start to pant.

"I am doing whatever you have done to me, the past few mornings, before I woke up." He lowered his head to nip her earlobe. His wet tongue traced the inside of her ear, and then the back of it, sending shivers down her body.

She wrapped her hands around his back and ran her fingers along his spine. He trembled in sharp reaction and bit her neck, while his hands kneaded her gorgeous breasts with a force that had built within him as he had eyed the alluring twin peaks over the past half hour.

When he plucked her nipples hard, she moaned loudly against his ear. He found that he loved her uncontrollable sexy voice. Lowering himself, he suckled the creamy mounds, using his tongue to flick and tease the sensitive nipples. Such a sweet taste!

She tore at his hair. Her body felt as if it were on fire, and her blood was rioting as it flowed down to her apex. When he wanted to move lower to worship her sex, she was eager for him. She parted her legs more widely and rubbed her legs against his hard shaft with frantic enthusiasm.

He let out a groan and gave in, pulling one of her knees to his waist. When he positioned himself and thrust into her decisively, she was tight. Very tight. He had never felt such intense pleasure before, from the friction and heat of her wet core.

Pushing deeper and deeper, he broke through her virginal barrier and joined with her, as one body. She gasped from the sharp pain, but soon her aroused breathing urged him on. When she wrapped both her legs around his waist, he started the maddening dance, drawing in and out. He savoured her sweet scent, her smooth, tight muscles and her rhythmic cries. As he thrust and pounded, his head was spinning with pleasure, and they both reached ecstasy at the same moment.

When they had caught their breath, he apologised for his initial remark. In turn, she told him her story, explaining the desire to save her elderly father that had prompted her to volunteer in his place.

Darcy laughed out loud when he heard about the rumours of the war.

"But, my love, the River Thames was pink because my bloody cousin, Richard The Blue Wizard, who is warring against me, overturned a ship which contained his pink virility potion."

"And the remains of the red coats in Hoyden Park?" Elizabeth asked.

"Richard hated me for besting him over a game of darts and in drinking. In a fit of pique, he tore up any uniforms of our army that he could find, and then directed his man to trample on them in Hoyden Park."

"But where have all the men in the kingdom gone?" she asked, not understanding.

"All are here in Londonland, drinking and learning how to throw darts. They compete with Blue Witch's men every day and night. I only play him once a year. So far, I've won for the past two years."

"Men and their vices!" Elizabeth exclaimed.

"Well, the darts and the drinking war will come to an end soon. Richard the Blue Wizard and I have agreed on a best-of-three-over-five-games rule. I only need to win over him this year and then all of the men can return to their homes. You have such a pair of fine eyes, I am sure you can teach my men better dart-throwing skills. And you can certainly drink most men under the table. I am confident that we can win over the Blue."

True to his words, General Darcy and Colonel Bennet triumphed over the Blue Wizard, in the end. All of the men were discharged and sent back to their homes. When Elizabeth returned home to her family, she arrived with her husband General Darcy and her baby boy. They stayed for a few days and then went back to Pemberley, Darcy's estate, where they lived happily ever after.

Lydia blamed her mother for forbidding her to go into the army. She was jealous of her sister's good fortune, as Lydia now preferred a bare chest and leather kilt to a red coat.

What if action of Pride and Prejudice had played out not in England but in Egypt?

PRAYER TO ISIS

1435BC, Merytum, Lower Egypt

Da, I will not forgive you this time, Elibeth swore as the boat left Merytum and sailed downstream. She was once again been married off to an upper-class husband without her consent, this time to a provincial leader no less.

Brokered into marriage by her money-tight parents at the age of fourteen, and again at eighteen, her two previous marriages had been carried out only by proxy. Her first husband died in a shipping accident, and the second died in a military expansion, before either of them could actually meet their bride. After that, she had thought that she was safely done with having to live with strange families for months on end; she had been certain that she would spend the rest of her life contently at home.

But she was not that fortunate. Her mother was in want of money again, and had apparently set her husband to marry Elibeth off again. Therefore, at the age of twenty-one, she was once again on a journey to the home of a strange family, the Darcymose.

Darcymose was the provincial leader at Pemberlium, one of the richest administrative regions of the Egyptian Kingdom. His family had governed the lush region for hundreds of years and reported to the vizier, the Pharaoh's second in command.

Normally, the great provincial leader would not have considered Elibeth, a poor engineer's daughter, to be suitable. But her last two marriages to men of great importance had elevated her status.

Still, she did not understand why he chose her. She had heard that many of the wealthy families in the kingdom had been attempting to marry their daughters into the Darcymose's family since the provincial leader turned fifteen. He was rumoured to be quite tall and handsome. But he had never married…until now. Her mother told her that he was on business in Upper Egypt, that explained why he wanted them to be married by proxy.

Elibeth would have lashed out at her father if he had been brave enough to face her. But no, she had only learned of the wedding from her mother half an hour before the ceremony, and she had then been shipped off immediately.

She thought back on the ceremony with anger. What an irony that she had been married in the Temple of Isis, the goddess of fertility, with Darcymose's familial priest presiding…and no sign of a bridegroom. Again. While the priest was praying for her to be blessed with many children, she was praying that Darcymose might greet his god of death, Anubis, before meeting her.

When she arrived at Pemberlium, she was stunned to learn that her husband had returned and was awaiting her in their quarters.

"You!" Elibeth hissed, reeling with shock upon seeing her new husband, for this was a man she had first met nearly three years earlier, at her second husband's home. At that time, he had been introduced to her as a friend of the family.

Darcymose stood and tried to wrap his arms around her waist in greeting, but she pushed him away. "Why did you use the name of 'Wenamun' and not Darcymose when we first met?" she demanded.

"Wenamun was my mother's surname." Darcymose said. "My father had just passed away, at that time. I did not want women fawning over me."

She thought back at the grim countenance he had often shown at that time, and felt a tinge of sympathy. "I did not know," she said. "I am sorry."

He pulled her with him, urging her to sit on the edge of the bed, and she allowed him to do so.

"But why did you marry me?" she asked in bewilderment. "Did you not say, back then, that my maidenhead might not be breakable because I was cursed? That, since my first husband had died before he could have a taste of my lips, the same would probably come true for my second husband, as well?"

He held her hands and rubbed them gently. Gazing down at her, he said, "I fell in love with you then. Of course I wished your second husband dead."

A shiver ran through Elibeth's body. "How could you fall in love with me? We only dined and talked together a few times."

"We danced once, as well."

His fingers left her palms and smoothed their way up her arms. She felt a warm current flowing through her body. "But that was three years ago."

"I had to allow a respectable amount of time to pass before I claimed you. I did not want your previous family to think we had formed an attachment back then. They would complain to the vizier and complicate the matter. But I have been keeping a close eye on your family. Had your mother wanted to marry you off sooner, I would have initiated my plan immediately." His hands reached her shoulders, and he used his thumbs to make circular motions at the base of her neck.

"I did not wish to marry again." She trembled, feeling the coarse texture of his thumbs and breathing in his musky scent. "What if I fight you?"

He remembered their last encounter. She had just heard about the death of her husband, and had seemed extremely relieved to know that she would soon be leaving that family. He recalled that, after drinking a few glasses of wine at dinner, her face had turned a lovely shade of pink.

He had rejoiced in the news for he known her husband was a violent man and that she would soon be freed, and so he himself had consumed a bit more than he should, as well. When he met her in the garden later that night, he could not suppress his ardent feelings, and kissed her passionately.

Taken by surprised, she had tried to struggle at first, but his lips soon persuaded her. By the time he parted her tunic and suckled her nipples, she was lost in the moment. She enjoyed his magical tongue and lips, feeling a pulse pounding between her thighs.

Only when he pushed his hands under her clothes and cupped her womanhood did sanity returned to her. She would not cheat on her husband on the day of his death, no matter how strongly she was attracted to this handsome man. And so she pushed him away.

He stood back at once, but extended his hand to touch her creamy mounds one last time. She, however, would have none of it, and slapped his face before running out of the garden.

Thinking back now on her temper and the fiery glint in her eyes, he was eager to provoke her passions once again. "You are welcome to fight me," he teased. Putting a hand on her shoulder, he grasped the front of her dress and tugged one side of it open. "But in bed only."

She gasped and raised her hand to strike him,

Anticipating her response, he caught her hand and lowered his head to kiss her wrist. Then he traced his lips down her arm and then across her breast until he reached her exposed nipple.

When he used his lips to pull her nipple taut, then wet the tight-gathered tip with his tongue, all strength left her body, and she subsided onto the bed.

He followed her lush body down and pushed the other side of the dress off her shoulder, baring her white alabaster breasts to his burning gaze. With three years of longing and ardency to fuel him, he devoured her creamy mounds, licking, suckling and squeezing them.

As his mad ministrations continued, the temperature in her body grew. She had never known such passion before. She tore at his hair, pressing him to her chest, then thrashed her head from side to side in sensual torment. She loved his torturing kisses but she wanted more, so much more...

She felt his hands leave her body as he struggled to strip off his clothes, and she whimpered in protest. He caught her nipple in his teeth in response. She screamed in ecstasy and reached her peak in that instant, trembling violently and feeling a wave of honey-sweet sensation at her apex. Then she went limp, as if floating on a cloud.

He quickly stripped off his clothes and returned to her. When he pressed his naked flesh against her hot skin, he felt that he had come home. He rubbed rhythmically against her, calling her urgently back from her bliss.

His hands kneaded her, dispensing with her gown, awakening every inch of her gorgeous body. Her breathing quickened again, and she parted her thighs instinctively to welcome his body.

He needed no additional encouragement. Guiding her legs to wrap around his waist, he pushed into her hot core with a forceful thrust, claiming her.

She moaned aloud as his hard shaft tore through her maidenhead and continued inward to press against her inner muscles. Panting hard, she felt him drive deeper and deeper, until he had reached her very hilt. Then he pulled out quickly, almost to the entrance, creating a burning sensation on her skin, before pounding into her with vigor once again.

She screamed in ecstasy as her inner muscles were stretched and rubbed by the passage of his throbbing manhood, in and out, on and on. Her hands dug into the muscles of his back, squeezing them hard when he was deep inside her and caressing them softly when he retreated to her entrance.

His muscular torso pressed and tantalised her twin peaks as his body drove up and down against her own. His lips kissed her earlobe as her teeth bit into his shoulder. Sweat against sweat, moan against moan, kiss against kiss, they strove.

He plunged into her for what seemed like ages, continuing long after she reached her peak of delight. Only when her fingernails traced his bottom and then teased at the juncture of his laboring thighs did he surrender and explode, crying out in utter satisfaction as he filled her with his seed. Completed, they trembled and convulsed together as one soul.

***

Was Elibeth's prayer in the Temple of Isis answered? Fortunately not.

Her third husband, Darcymose, lived to an old age and blessed her with many children. He could be rough and wild at some times, yet gentle and deeply tender at others. Although she did not love him in the beginning, she soon learned of his good character and became happy in her love of her husband soon thereafter.

As time went on, there could be seen in the gallery hall of Pemberlium many touching portraits and statues of their family, including children and grandchildren, revealing their marital delight and the warmth within their entire family, a happy history on display for the delight and inspiration of future generations.

What if Mr. Darcy was cursed?

THE DRAGON GENTLEMAN

Colonel Elizabeth Bennet surveyed the number of offerings with keen interest. Although her job was well remunerated, she still loved a bargain. She wanted to buy a robotic pet, this time. Since her sister Jane had married and moved out, she felt that her space station was a bit too quiet.

"Eliza!" The high pitch voice of Lt. Colonel Bingley gave her a shudder. "Did you have a good Christmas break?"

"Yes, great. And you, Lieutenant Colonel Bingley?" Elizabeth inquired politely, making a mental note of the fact that Caroline didn't address her as 'Colonel,' as she should. On the other hand, Elizabeth's sister Jane was now married to Caroline's brother Charles, making them sisters-in-law.

"Looking for a Christmas bargain? How about this miniature laser gun? It's cheap enough to be within your budget," Caroline said with a smirk.

Elizabeth's lips thinned. The lower-ranking officer came from a wealthy family, and she never let Elizabeth forget that her brother had 'lowered' himself to marry Jane.

"I don't need a gun, off duty." Elizabeth said, and moved on as a robotic green dragon some ten feet in height caught her fancy.

"What can this dragon do?" Colonel Bennet asked the captain in the sales ring.

"This is Dragon Wickham, made of titanium alloy. It can fly, and it can also arrange laundry or papers, due to its colour differentiation IQ."

Elizabeth pressed the muzzle of the dragon and it spoke. "Good day, Sir."

"It's not very intelligent. It can't distinguish my gender," Elizabeth remarked to the captain.

"Maybe because you don't look like a woman," Caroline said, intruding upon the conversation. Elizabeth had to admit that her sister-in-law dressed more femininely and provocatively, in leather vest and matching skirt, laced together. The flesh of Caroline's medically perfected breasts and hips was on display.

Elizabeth was traditional. She had never gone through plastic surgery, and so her body was not in symmetry.

Caroline pressed the muzzle of Dragon Wickham, and it greeted her by saying, "Lovely day, my dear." She snickered at Elizabeth with a triumphant smile.

"What is your intelligence makeup?" Elizabeth asked the dragon robot, sincerely interested. She wouldn't allow the annoying Caroline to distract her .

"Sir, I've an IQ of 138. I aim to serve, please and deliver for my master. Would you like a lick job on your tired legs?" Dragon Wickham inquired, and flapped its gigantic green wings as it circled around the two women.

Elizabeth laughed. It had a wicked sense of humour that she found quite charming. After a few more questions, she decided that it's not very smart but was great fun. She wrote her price down on her iComp, as she intended to bid for it.

Caroline leaned forward and stole a glance at the figure Elizabeth had written, determined to bid for this robotic pet, too.

She was furious that her brother had married Elizabeth's sister, causing them to be related. Caroline was richer, prettier and taller. The fact that Elizabeth had been made a Colonel at the young age of 20 didn't necessarily mean that she was smarter than Caroline.

Ever since Colonel Bennet had overtaken Caroline's rank earlier in the year, the latter had vowed to annoy her, whenever she had a chance. Now, Caroline was determined to buy up everything Elizabeth wanted.

As her rival walked on, Caroline was distracted by some shimmering feathers. The rainbow-coloured headpiece would complement her black leather gear quite well...

Elizabeth was happy she had managed to lose the annoying Caroline. She moved on and was looking at an e-Fan, a computer-assisted cooling device, when someone addressed her.

"Colonel, I'm a far better pet dragon than Wickham."

Elizabeth turned to see a small oriental dragon, gold in colour, sitting alone by the corner of the Intelligent Machine section.

"How do you know my rank? You're not considered a pet dragon anyway," Elizabeth murmured.

"With an IQ of 300, I'm classified as an Intelligent Machine. But I can be your pet robot."

This dragon was only about a foot long. Elizabeth thought it look too sad and serious for her liking, but she did like talking with a more intelligent pet, so she didn't rule it out. At least, not yet. And she liked its deep, smooth voice, as well.

"I knew your ranking because I'm equipped with a scanning device that enabled me to see your uniform and compare it to the information in my database."

Elizabeth nodded with approval.

"What can you do, then?" she asked.

"Everything Dragon Wickham can do and more."

Elizabeth was amused by the little dragon's reply and teased it. "Do you have a personal vendetta against the giant dragon?"

"We were made by the same manufacturer, at around the same time, but he's always too charming for my tastes."

"It can serve, please and deliver," Elizabeth stated, challenging the tiny dragon with its rival's abilities.

"He's best able to please his masters with his bright green colour, gigantic size and silver tongue, for those who are into outward appearance," the little dragon said dismissively.

"And you're not into that?"

"I'm deeper than that. I promise loyalty, honesty and responsibility to my masters."

Elizabeth nodded at this further sign of the tiny dragon's intelligence.

"You look rather lonely," it observed. "I'm good with heart-to-heart chat, should you feel so inclined."

She raised her eyebrows. Perhaps it was too smart for her.

"I compared your facial expression to my database, and deduced that you're smart, decisive, lonely, pretty…"

Her mouth curled up. Definitely too smart.

"Can you fly?" she asked. "You don't have wings like Dragon Wickham."

"I'm an oriental dragon. I use the strength of my long tail to fly."

She looked at it sceptically. It's so tiny that she's unsure how it defined a 'long' tail.

But the dragon lifted off suddenly and landed on her shoulder. "Pick me, Colonel Bennet. You won't regret it," it whispered in her ear, blowing warm air against her earlobe, making her shiver pleasantly.

"What's your name?" she asked, a bit unsettled by its action.

"Dragon Darcy. And I'm a male dragon."

She nodded. It – *he* – was strangely arrogant, but interesting enough, and so she wrote down a figure, half of what she was prepared to pay for Dragon Wickham.

Dragon Darcy then flew back to his stand and gave her a serious gaze.

At the end of the day, Caroline bought the huge Dragon Wickham and brought him back to her space station with a smug grin. Elizabeth shrugged her shoulders, untroubled at being outbid by Caroline.

On reflection, Elizabeth had decided that Dragon Darcy was quite special, and had purchased him. She seldom saw any oriental dragons. Most pet robots were western dragons.

"Welcome to Longbourn." Elizabeth talked to Darcy.

"It's comfortable, despite its size."

She arched her eyebrows, not sure that she should accept such a condescending tone from her pet.

"Let me pack up your sister's things. You can redecorate the station to your taste," Darcy said, and flew off to attend to the chore.

"You're too smart for your own good!" Elizabeth called after him. But she smiled. She and Jane did indeed have different tastes, so the decoration in the station was a compromise. Since Jane had moved out, she had intended for some time to revamp the decorating scheme to one that was more to her taste. It seemed that Darcy's database was extremely discerning. He could read her emotions, or perhaps even her thoughts.

He turned and brushed his mouth, with its delicate whiskers and beard, against her cheek. "You would be bored to death with me in two days if I weren't so smart."

She laughed out loud and pushed him away.

So the majestic tiny Dragon Darcy settled in at Longbourn, welcoming Elizabeth home after her hard day at work. He was handy in domestic chores like cooking, washing, repairing the plumbing and many more. He also became her confidante, offering her views and opinions on topics ranging from climate change, power struggles to the annoyance of her mother.

"What did Mrs. Bennet do this time?" Dragon Darcy greeted the Colonel. He could see that her eyes were flashing with frustration.

"She fixed me up with a blind date."

"You don't want to find a husband?"

"Colonel Collins is a toad, and I've suffered through two hours of his silly conversation."

"Too slimy?"

"Stupid, like a lap dog to his commanding officer."

"I thought obedience was a recommended quality in the army," he argued.

"Obedience is one thing. Smoothing the senior's ego is another."

"Flattery gets people into better places."

"Unfortunately, yes. And Mother said that if I don't settle down now, I won't find any man willing to marry me when I reach the rank of General. What a stupid notion! It's the 30th century. A woman doesn't need a man to make her life full anymore. I can use vibrators, or buy a man-whore robot to satisfy myself. And there are clinics, if I want children."

"True, but the journey of falling in love and finding a soul mate is worth it," he countered.

"What do you know about love?" she demanded.

"I know more than you might think," he replied in a wistful tone of longing.

"Ah, your intelligent database again," she said, and shook her head.

"Let's forget about this slimy toad. I'll draw you a bath."

As Elizabeth lay in the lavender-scented bubbles, she felt the stress of the blind date and the frustration with her mother disappear. She was glad of Darcy's attention to detail.

"Thanks, Darcy," she said and closed her eyes.

"Don't mention it." He flew in and out of the water, dipping and lifting the bubbles, messing it around the bathroom and all over her hair.

"Stop it!" she protested, and laughed.

He flew near her and used his whiskers and beard to nuzzle her nose.

"Naughty!" She grabbed him by the waist, preventing him from flying off. Suddenly their eyes met, and they gazed at each other intently.

"Thank you, Darcy, for cheering me up. I love you," she said, then pulled the dragon toward her and kissed his nose.

Blast!

Suddenly, she felt the scales on Darcy's body vibrate, and she lost her grip on the tiny dragon. Her eyes widened as she saw Dragon Darcy's skin burst open as the foot-long dragon began to grow larger. His body elongated alarmingly, both in length and in girth.

By the time he had grown to roughly six feet, Elizabeth had scrambled out of the bath tub and plastered herself against the wall, too shocked to utter a word.

Then Darcy's tail seemed to lose the strength to hold his bigger body aloft, and he dropped into the bubble bath with a big splash.

"Darcy, are you alright?" Elizabeth cried out and hurried to the edge of the tub.

The water stirred and whirled at high speed, and the bubbles became murky. She was preparing to dip her hands into the water in search of her pet robot when his head abruptly emerged from under the bubbles.

He shook off the water and looked at Elizabeth.

She gaped at him, astonished. Dragon Darcy was no longer a dragon.

"Elizabeth," he said, in his normal deep voice.

"Darcy? Is this…you?"

"Yes."

"But how could you turn into…a man?"

"I was cursed, nearly two hundred years ago." He blinked away the water and pushed himself up from the tub. "Rather like the prince and the frog."

"Cursed? By whom?"

"Witch Catherine de Bourgh."

Elizabeth gaped. "Truly? Why?"

"I refused to marry her sickly daughter. I was hoping to marry for love."

"You poor thing!" she exclaimed.

But he was not a poor thing at all. Elizabeth's mouth still showed a tendency to hang open, for he was an exquisite specimen of a male human being. Around six feet five inches tall, he had broad shoulders, a hard six-pack, a pert butt and masculine legs, not to mention an extremely well-endowed manhood.

He also sported a beard and long hair. As he brushed the scales from his body, she couldn't drag her gaze away from his naked form.

He stopped midway through brushing away the scales on his shaft when he caught her looking at him with sparkling eyes.

"You broke the curse when you kissed me and said that you loved me. I'm all yours from now on," he said with a grin.

"All mine?"

"Yes. Your pet, your servant, your man-whore…and your husband, if you will have me."

She was speechless but tempted. She licked her lips and gazed at him intensely.

Darcy took over decisively. Picking her up, he carried her to the bedroom. "I haven't slept with a woman for two hundred years. I've a lot to catch up on, if you're willing," Darcy said, and with that he lowered his mouth and kissed her tenderly.

At the young age of twenty, Elizabeth had not yet slept with a man, so she was nervous. But she reminded herself that she had known him for half a year. She genuinely liked him, his arrogance, intelligence, sensitivity and all. Since he said he would be hers from now on, who was she to pass on such a chance to use him for a bit of fun?

She ran her fingers along his neck, then smoothed her palms over his shoulders and back, then down to his tightly muscled bottom. Occasionally, she still encountered a scale or two, tangible reminders to her that he had so recently been a dragon. But as Darcy trailed hot, wet kisses from her ear to her collarbone, and down to her breasts, she shivered with anticipation.

His tongue was magical. He licked and twirled around her aureole, first on one breast, then on the other, making them peak. Then his teeth gently pulled at the hardened nipples. She felt a mixture of pain and pleasure race down to the apex of her thighs.

She moaned aloud as he used his fingers to caress her nub and folds. When he pushed a finger into her core, then two, thrusting in and out, preparing her for what was to come later, she screamed to her climax within minutes.

He didn't stop there. While her heart was still pumping fast, her inner muscles still pulsing, she felt him move lower to worship her sex with his mouth.

In an instant, she was burning again. She twisted and thrust her sensitised body to avoid his magical mouth but he held her hips to still her. His tongue lapped up her juice and pushed into her core. In between thrusts of his tongue, his lips nipped at her hidden bud, rubbing it to swollen ripeness.

Her moans became louder and louder until he drove her over the edge with his hard, clever tongue. Her body jerked up and down as the ecstasy of orgasm exploded in her body.

Only then did he slide his thick shaft into her, in a single mighty thrust. Her body was swimming in the afterglow of two climaxes, And she felt no pain at all when he broke through her barrier.

Knowing that he had stretched and strained her inner muscles, he held still, allowing her to grow used to the presence of his burning, throbbing rod within her, while his hands and mouth returned to tease and pleasure her lips and breasts.

When she began to pant and squirm hungrily again, he resumed his movements in her. He raised and lowered his body, slowly at first, coaxing until she reciprocated the same actions. He thrust and she squeezed. He withdrew and she raised her hips. Their intimate slow dance turned into quick steps very soon. He pounded into her, impaling her, with the eagerness of a thirsty man who has travelled across the desert without water and finally found the oasis. He drank in her scent, her juice and her essence with every frenetic thrust of his shaft.

But Darcy stopped as she neared the peak, and allowed her to slide back to a calmer plateau. Then he repeated the journey and brought her to the brink again. Her nails dug into his back as he lifted her up and down, raging through the valleys and mountains of sexual exploration again and again.

It felt as if the journey took ages. Elizabeth was at the sixth or seventh near-peak when she took control, tracing her fingertips along his spine and down into the crease of his butt, thus pushing him over the edge. She rode him, pulsing and shivering, and reached her peak at last.

They convulsed and vibrated in unison, crying aloud in ecstasy as he spilled his boiling seed into her, sealing their love.

***

Once Dragon Darcy was freed of the curse, there was no holding him back. He retained his intelligence and integrated into modern society with Elizabeth's help. Elizabeth, in her turn, found that she didn't want him to be her pet or servant. They soon married, and he joined the galaxy army, as well. Within two short years, husband and wife reached the rank of General together.

Lieutenant Colonel Caroline Bingley had tried to discover where Elizabeth met her magnificent husband. But she never uncovered the truth, beyond the simple fact that they had met during the galaxy Christmas bargain sales.

After several failed attempts to seduce Darcy, which resulted in her being humiliated by the silent treatment of the couple, she finally gave up. She lived alone, accompanied only by her pet dragon robot Wickham. She lamented, after all, that she had not really found so fine a bargain as had that annoying Eliza.

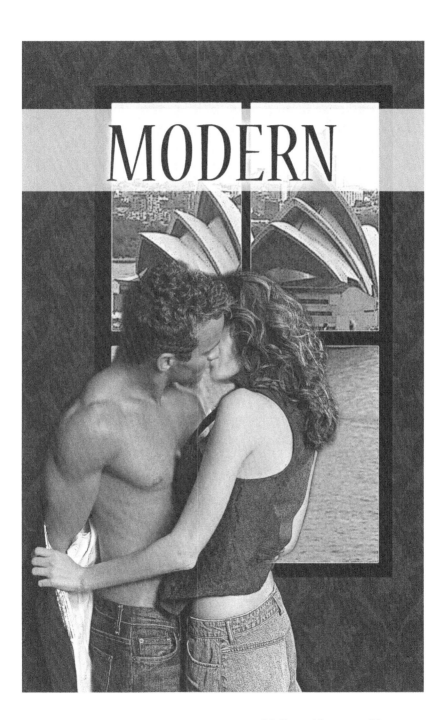

MODERN

What if Mr. Darcy had an odd friend?

THREE INCHES

Looking through window at the pristine snow, Elizabeth Bennet gave a deep sigh. The tranquility of the natural scenery didn't ease her mind. It was her fifth day of work at Pemberley Ski Resort, near Wilder Kaiser in Austria. She knew she shouldn't be here, but she couldn't make herself to leave. After all, what was the chance of her meeting him ever again, even though this was one of his most famous business ventures?

She thought about their roller coaster "relationship". *Did we actually have a relationship?* she asked herself.

William Darcy and she had met in a tennis class in Sydney. Staying there to oversee a business merger for a few months, he had taken time out in the evening, joining the local suburban tennis class. The facility and the coach, though not first class, seemed quite professional to Elizabeth.

But she overhead him talking to his friend, Charles Bingley, snickering at the sub-standard coach, the poorly maintained court and the hopeless fellow players – like herself. "She's tolerable, I suppose," he said, "but not good enough to play a mixed double with me." Those had been his exact words. Who did he think he was? Rafael Nadal? Roger Federer?

To her utmost satisfaction, she'd had a great time showing him how good she was, playing a mixed double against him. Wickham and she demolished Caroline Bingley and the arrogant man in a 6-2, 6-1 win. Since then, Darcy had been glaring at her, eavesdropping on her conversations with others all the time.

Besides seeing each other in court, Charles was dating Elizabeth's sister, Jane, and so Darcy and she saw each other frequently. She soon learned that his sneering attitude extended to her mother and younger sisters. He found them noisy, crude and vulgar.

Offended by his pompous manner, she took every opportunity to taunt and tease him. Busily triumphing over her success at goading him, she was utterly unprepared, one night soon after the match, for his sudden declaration of love and lust.

They were trying to recover a lost ball in the bushes besides the tennis court when he suddenly pressed her against a tree and kissed her senseless. His tongue and hands were like magic, setting her whole body on fire. Forgetting about his conceited behaviour, she responded passionately to his advances.

When they stopped for air, he declared himself to have been madly in love and in lust with her since their first meeting. He asked her back to his place to continue the "mutual groping". At that, her wit returned, and she lashed out at his arrogance, conceit and haughtiness. She told him that he would be the last man she would shag, especially since learning about his involvement in persuading Bingley to dump Jane, and about his mistreatment of Wickham, his old friend.

In anger, she tried to leave, but he grabbed her arms, wanting to explain. She ended up shoving her knee against his balls, leaving him to cry in pain.

A few days later, however, it was she who was crying, for having misjudged him.

He retreated to London and sent her an email to explain everything: He had talked to Charles and found out what happened. He did ask his friend to cool down the fast romance and make sure of where his heart was. He didn't know that Charles's sister Caroline would spread vile lies, persuading Charles that Jane had moved on to a bigger fish.

He also explained his dealings with Wickham, who was involved in drugs, women and gambling. He even provided evidence of how Wickham had schemed money from Darcy's sister, Georgiana, and broken her young and innocent heart.

A few weeks after Darcy's explanation, Bingley had returned to Sydney and made up with Jane. Elizabeth also berated herself for listening to Wickham, a mere casual acquaintance she had met at the tennis club, over someone she had grown to know much better over more than a month's time.

But did she really know Darcy better? How could she not have noticed that he loved her? How could she forget his gaze, his tolerant smile over her teasing, his subtle catering to her wishes when they were together, and his occasional brushing of his hand over her arms, her fingers, her back? Looking back, they all made sense now.

She regretted not staying to hear him out and to resolve her misunderstanding. She was sorry for hurting him, both physically and mentally. He had confessed that he had been an awkward teenager, and that he hadn't expected to grow tongue-tied and feel a lack of confidence again when he fell in love with her. He was sorry to have forced his passion on her, and he understood why she found him lacking...

Elizabeth found that she could read his anger, sadness, love and resignation in his email.

Did she regret him? Certainly he was smart, tall and sizzling hot. But those were simply external attributes. Could she truly fall for a stuck-up snob who looked down on everyone?

As a result of those questions and uncertainties, she had never replied to his email. But now, up on the mountain, she was finally receiving her answer.

Darcy was no snob. He had been a caring brother and compassionate soul to everyone at Pemberley Ski Resort and in the surrounding little villages.

He had come here in his early twenties, and had happened upon a devastating avalanche. Several villages were covered by the snow, with lives lost and businesses destroyed. He helped Mrs. Reynolds, who lost her entire family in the accident, to rebuild her home. He donated a great deal of money and devoted many weeks each year to helping the community. He opened his resort here as a means of regenerating growth in the area. And he did it right. The place was prosperous and full of happy laughter now, and nearly everyone Elizabeth met had a glowing story to tell about Mr. Darcy.

She had no chance of seeing him again; indeed, Mrs. Reynolds said that he was not expected at the Resort for the remainder of the winter. Isolated from him, however, Elizabeth understood for the first time that she might actually have been attracted to him, right from the beginning. That would explain her indignation over his slight, as well as her constant attempts to tease him in an attempt to spark a reaction from him. It also explained why she liked being with him, and why she had kissed him back so passionately.

She sighed again, then decided to earn her keep by opening the letters that had just been delivered by the postman: bills, junk mail, bookings and more bills. None of it interested her…until she came upon a pink envelope with a card inside, addressed to Mr. William Darcy and marked 'private.'

Tomorrow would be Valentine's Day. Could this be a Valentine's card from his present girl friend? Did he have a lover now? Why had it been sent here?

Elizabeth racked her brain, thinking hard. She had been feasting on gossip magazines since she arrived, but she hadn't seen any recent photos of him with any women.

"Private, but not personal. I'm the secretary here…" she murmured. Curiosity was killing her. After a few minutes of deliberation, she decided to open the card.

It was a cheap, bland Valentine's card with a red heart on the front. Inside were a few short sentences of nearly illegible writing, marred with many blots:

My dear Darce,

I t's time of the y ear. Get your 3 inches out and s hag some girls wit less.

Ig ore their comp ains and en joy yourself!

Your best friend

B

"Shit!" Elizabeth dropped the card and swore, "What did Bingley tell him to do?" She picked up the card and read it again, with growing indignation. "Get your 3 inches out and shag some girls witless? Ignore their complaints and enjoy yourself? What sort of best friend is Bingley? Should I tell Jane about it? Why would any girl want to complain if Darcy shags her? I certainly wouldn't complain. The man is scorching hot! But hang on! 3 inches! What does he mean, 3 inches? How many centimetres is that?"

Elizabeth scratched her head and wished she had done better in class with mathematics. She hated the imperial system. Luckily, Google was right in front of her. She typed in "length converter" and clicked on the first website.

Three inches = 7.62 centimetres.

She looked at the ruler on her desk, right in front of her eyes. Surely that couldn't be! Such a hot guy couldn't be so badly endowed. He was tall, and his hands and feet were big. His shoulders were broad, his biceps strong. She thought back to their tennis lessons. He usually wore loose sport trousers, so there was no way she could tell about…other measurements. Anyway, she had not ogled him. Well…that wasn't entirely true. She might have ogled him a little bit – his legs and torso. But not there!

I understand why you found me lacking…

She thought back to what he had written in his email. Could it be true? "Oh, I'm so sorry, Mr. Darcy!" she whispered in sympathy.

"What are you sorry about, Elizabeth?" asked a deep voice from behind her, making her jump.

Elizabeth shoved the card into the pocket of her jeans, turned and saw Darcy's big frame silhouetted in the doorway. He was encased in a thickly layered ski suit, but she could still see his muscular physique, handsome face and soulful eyes.

"I…," She gasped, then gathered her courage and gave him a bright smile. "I didn't find you lacking. Will you give me a second chance? You know…for the mutual …groping."

His eyes widened and his pupils dilated. Taking her hand, he led her out of the office to his room, at the far end of the resort.

While they walked hand in hand, she vowed to show him her love and to make certain that he enjoyed himself, despite of his deficiency.

He led her into his room, pressing her against the door the moment they were inside, not sparing any time to switch on the light. He gave her a sizzling hot kiss, nipping at her upper lip and then thrusting his tongue against hers. It traced an erotic path along her inner muscles, making her blood flow rapidly through her body and pool at her apex.

On and on, he caressed her mouth, pouring his longing from the past few months into the kiss.

His cold hands tore at the buttons on her blouse and her front-clipped bra, winning access to her sumptuous breasts. As his fingers puckered her nipples into hard peaks, his tongue drove even more deeply into her mouth. She felt nearly choked by his violent action.

Grasping his shoulders, she dug her fingers into his back. As if sensing her vulnerability, he slowed the tempo. His hands began to shape, palm, knead and fondle her twin peaks tenderly, while his tongue made love to her mouth slowly.

The fluid of arousal flowed through her, and she felt herself reaching the peak. Shivered violently, she climaxed, still standing with her back to the door. As her legs weakened, she nearly collapsed onto the floor.

Breaking from the kiss, he picked her up and placed her on his bed. His mouth moved quickly, drawing an alluring path from her lips down her throat, then between her deep cleavage and on to her navel.

Then his hands made quick work of her jeans, taking them and the panties off in one go. He marveled at her lush body in front of his eyes. Parting her legs, he lowered his mouth and slid his tongue along her folds, while his thumb rubbed her bud.

Her body bucked under his ministrations, but his strong hands shifted to hold her hips on the bed. With his forceful tongue, he thrust into her wet entrance, invading her hot inner core. She squirmed and moaned aloud, begging him to relieve her suffering.

He was merciless in his attack. He suckled her bud and thrust his tongue in and out, on and on until she screamed out in abandon, reaching her second orgasm.

In its aftermath, Elizabeth was in a haze as she noticed him stripping off his thick ski suit. Before she could see his body properly, he settled between her parted legs. She wrapped her hands around his neck, gazed at him and said, with a firm voice, "William, I love you, no matter what. Make me yours."

He returned her gaze and replied, "I love you, too, Elizabeth." Then he nudged her legs even further apart and thrust into her.

OMG, he was so big and thick! She nearly blurted out the words.

Even though she was fully aroused and wet to the core, she found her muscles stretched to the limited. She panted heavily as he pushed more and more into her. Every cell in her body was torched by his hot, hard shaft. His hands moved to her breasts again, squeezing them hard as she panted in response.

She instinctively raised her body and wrapped her legs around his waist to accommodate his invasion. With a sudden swift thrust of his body, he pushed right to the hilt, grazing the entrance to her womb with his tip.

Elizabeth's eyes rolled back, and she believed she was in heaven again. Then he began to move. He pulled away, right to her entrance, then rammed into her hard, pounded into her again and again. The sound from the encounter of their sweaty bodies, their moans and their cries, created a kind of sexually charged music in the room. To her astonishment, she realized that she could reach that higher paradise again.

After endless minutes of ardent thrusting, he finally drove into her with such a mighty surge that his tip fitted itself against her very core. At that, she cried out in ecstasy and reached her third peak, trembling and convulsing on and on, until she squeezed him so hard with her inner muscles that he shouted out in bliss. He shivered, poured his essence into her and collapsed on top of her.

When they finally returned to earth, he rolled away from her, then pulled her to lie on top of him. He switched on the bedside lamp, wanting to devour her lovely body with his eyes.

Her eyelids felt heavy but her gaze suddenly snagged on the sight of her jeans on the floor...and the pink envelop spilling out of the pocket.

Bewildered, she raised her head, took a look at his relaxed body, and asked him in wonder, "William, why did Charles send you a Valentine's card?"

He looked at her in confusion. "What are you talking about?"

"He said you only had 3 inches! But you're huge!" Then, embarrassed at discussing his size, she blushed and covered her cheeks with her hand.

"Oh. That," Darcy said as understanding dawned on him.

"I felt sorry for your..." Words failed her, and she raised her little finger to show him what she meant.

"You asked me to make love to you because you felt sorry about my ...?"

"No. I would have made love to you, no matter what. I love you." She lowered her head and kissed away his concerns.

When they stopped for air, he said, "The card wasn't from Bingley. It was Billy who wrote it."

"My cousin Mr. Collins? Why would he send you such a strange card?"

"I knew him in my teens. One year, he came to the Hunsford camp with my aunt. It was around Valentine's Day. He made out with a girl, one night. The next day, when we were both in the toilet, we overheard the girl outside, laughing about his size with some of her friends."

"Oh dear."

"Oh dear, indeed. He took a look at me and burst into tears, lamenting his small size. I comforted him, telling him that size didn't truly matter. I assured him that he would find someone who loved him for what he was. Since then, he has counted me as his best friend. He sends me a Valentine's card every year. He said we should encourage each other, in such a lonely time."

Elizabeth frowned. "But he said 'take your 3 inches out and shag some girls witless.' He was joking?"

Darcy's face turned bright red. "He said, back then, that I *looked to be* 9 inches. But you've seen his writing. He must have blotted the 9 into looking like a 3. I've received similar cards from him, in the past, each messier than the last."

"9 inches? That's nearly 23 centimetres," she murmured, and glanced at his lower body.

Their talk had clearly aroused him, for his manhood was standing tall and proud. Elizabeth stretched her small hand out, as if to measure it.

Darcy would have none of that and smacked her hand away. "If you want to measure it, I know a much better method." Rolled her onto her back, he thrust inside her again.

And that is how they came to spend the night and all of Valentine's Day measuring and discussing the relative merits of the metric system.

What if Mr. Darcy expressed himself on the occasion as sensibly and as warmly as a man violently in love might be supposed to do?

BEDROOM ABILITY

Elizabeth Bennet slowly awoke to the sound of a phone ringing, the caress of a man's strong hands on her breasts, and his growing hardness pressing importunately against her bottom.

One of his hands left her momentarily.

"Yes…No…Yes…Hmm…Ok…Bye." The sound of the man answering the call roused her from her lingering stupor, for it sounded like…Mr. Darcy!

She opened her eyes and stared straight ahead.

"Shit!" she swore under her breath, for what she saw was his office.

She lowered her glance as his tan, dark-haired arm settled back on her white breasts again.

From the waist up, she was without a stitch of clothing. And his big, hot hands were slowly rubbing and pinching her nipples.

She sucked in a deep breath and squirmed, then swore, "Shit," again as she felt his firm arousal prod her butt cheeks. She was *completely* naked, without anything covering the lower part of her body, either.

How did I get here? she wondered wildly.

The decorations in his office reminded her that it was Christmas. Events and images flashed through her mind: Caroline Bingley, the Human Resources dragon, laughing behind her back, the day before. The orange woman had snickered at her, saying that Elizabeth was a prim and proper tomboy who wore a buttoned-up shirt, trousers and short hair, a boring, fat lad who didn't know how to have fun with men.

After that, Elizabeth had shopped for the most alluring and feminine frock she could find, to shock the acid-tongue woman at the office Christmas party. With a constant supply of wine and champagne to bolster her courage, she had flirted and laughed with nearly every man in the company.

She remembered that her big boss hadn't seemed to like her new behaviour. When she saw Mr. Darcy withdraw from the festivities with a frown, she followed him into his office, determined to make her serious boss have some fun.

Actually, she had done a lot more than that. She remembered, after a bit of happy banter, how she had pushed him down to sit rigidly on the chesterfield couch, feeding him sips of bubbly from her own mouth until...

"Elizabeth, my love," Mr. Darcy murmured, close to her ear. His deep, velvety voice made her shiver. Then his tongue stroked her earlobe, before nipping and sucking on it.

She trembled. Her mind couldn't concentrate any more. As his hands squeezed and cupped her breasts to sensual heights, she panted and cried out in low moans.

Arching her body involuntarily, she felt one of his legs push hers at an angle. Granted access, his impressive shaft slid along her outer folds from behind, making her apex ablaze.

One of his hands left her twin peaks and travelled down to her pubic hair. His demanding fingers rubbed and tweaked her sensitized nub from the front. The dual attack rendered her instantly afire and soaking wet.

Elizabeth grabbed onto his arms, bracing herself as she felt him position himself at her entrance. When he pushed into her, stretched her tight and tender inner muscles insistently, she let out a loud moan.

This super-big boss of hers was jumbo-sized, invading her in a way she had never experienced before. She bit her lip and squeezed her eyes shut as sensation of friction and scorching heat spread through her core.

He pushed in, inch after inch, slowly, steadily, relentlessly, until at last he reached her hilt. Suddenly, she remembered this ecstasy of his manhood inside her, recalling it from the last time. She had been in control then, straddling him, using gravity and determination as she lowered herself onto his impressive girth. Panting, she had confessed to him she had never before done the deed in any way but the missionary position, on a proper bed. After she took control and fucked him wildly while he continued to sit stiffly on the sofa, she told him it had been the best sex she had ever had.

Now he was invading her from behind, filling her in places she didn't know could be filled, creating another unforgettable dream. But when he started to pull out and push into her rhythmically, building to a neck-breaking speed, she knew it was a wonderful reality instead.

His sizzling mouth was biting her neck. His burning hands had returned to pluck at her throbbing nipples while his blazing shaft pounded into her with maddening urgency. After endless minutes of amazing sensory assault, her body couldn't take it any more. She screamed out his name and dug her fingers deeply into his forearms as she rode out the highest climax she had ever reached. The waves of it crashed through her body for ages.

Still quivering with delight, she felt him pump into her in a frenzy of quick pulses and then freeze, his tip stopped at the depth of her womb. Growling savagely, he blasted his essence into her. His teeth bit into her shoulder, and his convulsions prolonged the orgasm she was still experiencing.

Her body was on fire, torched where their skin touched, where his mouth and hands stroked, and where his manhood throbbed. Her mind was satiated for a long time, and she whimpered in protest when he finally withdrew from her and turned her to lie on her back.

He brushed the wayward curls from her sweaty face and lowered his mouth to kiss her eyelids.

When she opened her eyes, she was greeted by the brightest of smiles on his face. His emerald gaze bored into her. The lovely dimples made him look like a young man of twenty, instead of a mature businessman of thirty five.

He smoothed his hands along her body, then lifted her left hand. He kissed each of her fingers, and a glinting light made her eyes widen.

"What…?" She swallowed hard.

"We're engaged, my love," he said, and leaned down to kiss her deeply.

She squirmed in astonishment, and accidentally pushed him off of the sofa.

He laughed and pulled her down on top of him, then rolled to pin her gently beneath him.

Once again, her concentration was broken by the sensation of his lips and tongue. He pressed his muscled frame against her on the rug, guiding her legs up to wrap around his waist, and she felt him spring to life again.

Is this man Superman? she wondered wildly as she wrapped her arms around his neck.

His tongue thrust into her mouth as his hard rod searched, shifted, and then impaled her anew. Her body was wet and ready, still hot from their last encounter. Insatiable, he plunged into her again and again, on and on, a dance of delirious delight.

This time, they reached their peak together. Their moans and groans filled the office and echoed in their ears. When he collapsed on top of her, she loved the feeling of connection with this big man.

Slowly, she returned to earth. He sat up to relieve her of his weight, and settled with his back to the chesterfield. Then he pulled her up to sit on his lap.

"You'll move in with me today, won't you?" His deep voice brought her back from the hazy clouds.

She gazed at him, finally remembering how, after their first coupling, he had pulled her to his desk, set her down on his chair and retrieved something from the top drawer. Kneeling in front of her, buck naked, he had proposed to his equally naked personal assistant.

"I've loved you passionately, since not long after you started working for me," he had explained. "I started carrying my mother's ring with me, this last month. The sparkles of the diamond remind me of your eyes."

She'd smiled at the unconventional proposal from her naked boss, then impetuously agreed. He, in turn, had slipped the beautiful diamond ring onto her finger and they'd celebrated with a tender and slow lovemaking, on his desk! He'd confided that it had been one of his fantasies for quite a while.

Wow, so he's fucked me senseless four times in the past few hours, Elizabeth now thought. Suddenly she remembered she had indeed been 'senseless', no doubt dulled by the alcohol. Didn't she dislike her arrogant boss?

"Umh...Mr. Darcy..." she stammered.

"William."

"Umh...William..." The rumbling of her stomach startled both of them. They stared at each other, then broke into chuckles. She had never seen him so carefree.

"We'd better feed you with food, too." He winked and pulled her to stand up.

While she was debating how to tell him that she'd been drunk when she agreed to his proposal, he dressed both her and himself quickly. He seemed very capable at slipping her into her bra and panties, and then sheathing her in her tight black cocktail dress.

Once that was done, he wrapped his hand around her waist and led her out of the office. As a young man violently in love, he chatted non-stop how much he loved her, all the way back to his townhouse in Knightsbridge. She found she couldn't edge in a word to hamper his enthusiasm.

His elderly housekeeper greeted them at the door.

"Mrs. Reynolds, you remember my personal assistant, Elizabeth Bennet?" He made the introduction warmly.

Elizabeth's face turned bright red as the elderly lady looked her up and down. Darcy still had his arm around her waist, and Elizabeth felt sure that Mrs. Reynolds knew they'd had sex, because Elizabeth's hair and dress were dishevelled.

"Miss Bennet. Merry Christmas."

"Mrs. Reynolds. Merry…Christmas." *Damn, why can't I talk normally?* Elizabeth thought. *Must be the effect of Mr. Darcy's hand rubbing my waist.*

"Elizabeth and I are engaged. She's moving in here. We're a bit hungry right now. Do you have any goodies?"

Oh, great! Now he's announced it to the world.

"Oh, William, that's wonderful news." Mrs. Reynolds gave him a kiss on the cheek before hugging Elizabeth tightly. "I've some sandwiches in the fridge. You didn't bring any personal belongings with you yet, Miss Bennet?"

"Mr. Darcy…William…rushed me here…"

"Of course I did! I didn't want her to change her mind about moving in." He winked and pulled her into the kitchen.

By the time they finished the sandwiches, another person came into the kitchen.

"Well, William, you certainly stayed at the office party a lot longer, this year," his sister said cheerfully. "What kept you?"

"My fiancée and I were…occupied." He smiled at Elizabeth, who felt her blush spread to her chest. *Did he have to tell everyone what they had just done?*

Georgiana squeaked and flung herself on him. "Congratulations, brother!"

"You remember Elizabeth Bennet, my personal assistant these last six months. My sister, Georgiana."

Georgiana then hugged Elizabeth warmly. "You can call me Gigi. And thanks for taking my dull and overbearing brother off my back."

"Georgiana!" he chastised.

She stuck her tongue out at him and continued talking to Elizabeth. "I didn't have much chance to talk to you, last time, but I've heard so much about you! He laughed over how you gave him a dressing down for bad dictation."

Elizabeth remembered the incident, which had transpired just three days after she started working for him. She had made a few mistakes in her typing, and he was furious with her. In turn, she had told him that she'd never had that kind of problem with her bosses before. She suggested that he dictate closer to the recorder, not with his head wandering around in every direction.

Darcy also remembered the incident. He had been annoyed with Caroline for hiring such a badly dressed personal assistant for him while he was away. He had only taken Charles's sister out a few times, to some business functions, but she seemed to think that she owned the company – and him!

After his initial attack on Elizabeth's taste in clothing, he had found her efficient, intelligent and refreshing. By the third day, he had begun to feel attracted to her. His gaze followed her everywhere, as he enjoyed the fantasy of stripping the hideous business suit and trousers off of her and doing wicked things to her voluptuous body everywhere in the office. That was the true reason why the quality of his dictation had slipped.

He'd scolded her for the typing mistakes but she, in turn, gave him a fiery dressing down. Her temper was refreshing. Since then, he had been in love with her. He hadn't asked her out on dates because they were working days and sometimes nights together anyway. And on the weekends, because her sister Jane was already dating his friend Charles, Darcy and Elizabeth often saw each other socially, as well.

He loved that she was unafraid of him, and that she didn't fawn over him. Instead, she spoke her mind, both professionally and socially. They often had heated but inspiring debates. He treated her more as a friend than as an employee. It had become more and more difficult for him to reframe from expressing his love to her, but he was still unsure of her family. Her mother and younger sisters sounded, and behaved, like gold diggers.

But when she'd turned up at the Christmas party dressed like a glamorous sex kitten, and had proceeded to flirt with every man there, he was jealous as hell. He resolved to talk to her after the Christmas party, then retreated to his office to calm the green-eyed monster. But she followed him into the office, where she not only told him but also showed him how to have fun.

And, boy, had he had fun! He had never been ridden by a wild woman before. Strangely, he found that he loved this domination by his petite love. He'd experienced the best climax of his life when she rode him to oblivion, and he was ecstatic when she agreed to marry him. Their subsequent love-making sessions had been as marvellous as the first one. He hadn't know that he was capable of shagging her four times in such a short span of time.

The phone rang again, and he answered it curtly. "Yes?…Wickham…hell…"

Elizabeth watched as Darcy stalked out of the kitchen to continue the conversation. Then Mrs. Reynolds excused herself, leaving Elizabeth to remember her other objection to him. Besides their initial clash at work, she had also heard George Wickham, a junior in admin, speak about how badly Darcy had mistreated him, preventing him from dating Georgiana.

"This Wickham…he's your boyfriend?" Elizabeth asked Georgiana.

"He was dreaming!" Georgiana exclaimed. "William and Wickham grew up together. I was much younger. When I was in junior high, Wickham wanted to date me. Come on, he's so old! Like my brother. Who would want an elderly brother as a date? Wickham made a nuisance of himself, and my brother told him that he would fire him if he continued. It took that to make his yucky behavior stop."

Elizabeth gritted her teeth. She had been taken in by a delusional stalker! *"Georgiana and I love each other so much, and her brother separated us. We vowed to keep our chastity till she reaches 21, and then run away together."* Those had been Wickham's melodramatic words. "Why did Mr. Darcy hire him in the first place? Just because they were friends?"

"Wickham is my father's godson, so William took care of him whenever he could. I told William he should have washed his hands of him ages ago. Godson, my ass!"

At that point, Darcy walked back into the kitchen. "Georgiana, good night. Elizabeth and I are tired." He arched his eyebrows at Elizabeth when he spoke. Then he pulled her upstairs, to his room.

So, what should I do now? she wondered. *He didn't mistreat Wickham. He might have been a bit arrogant in that dictation incident, but he's smart, serious and responsible. He loves me to bits, and he sure knows how to fuck me senseless…*

While she was still mentally debating the relative merits of keeping or breaking the engagement, he pulled her into the bathroom and started divesting them both of their clothes. In moments, she was a lost woman. Again.

When they married, six months later, she teased him that it was his bedroom ability that persuaded her to stay in the engagement long enough for her to fall in love with him.

He retorted that she had certainly taken her time, giving him ample opportunity to prove that his abilities extended to the office, the bathroom, the bedroom, and almost everywhere else inside his townhouse and country estate.

"Well," she answered, contented in his arms, "a good personal assistance ought to be thorough. Don't you agree?"

What if Mr. Darcy and Wickham had a fight?

BILLIONAIRE CONVICTED

People around the world were outraged that convicted billionaire William Darcy was given an unbelievably light sentence, serving only a day at Meryton's charity co-op, Ice Cream Vision.

"How difficult can it be to be an ice-cream taster? It's a dream job, not a punishment," a woman in London said.

"That rich brat must have bribed the fat judge at Meryton," a man from New York claimed.

On April 1st, 2008, Darcy pleaded guilty at Meryton Court to a charge of reckless assault against his former friend, George Wickham. Darcy was sentenced to one day of community service.

Computer whiz kid Darcy was staying with his friend, Charles Bingley, at Netherfield Mansion, in the town of Meryton a year ago, when the incident occurred. During a party hosted by Bingley, Wickham became drunk and verbally abused a local woman whose name was withheld from the press.

Darcy got involved in an altercation with Wickham about the woman, hitting Wickham on the face several times with an expensive pair of shoes, giving his victim a black eye and a bloody nose.

The Berluti boots, Rapieces Reprises, looked extremely stylish, especially with their innovative orange hue color. Sadly, they were an unwanted gift from Bingley's sister Caroline to the billionaire, with an original price tag of $1,830. She claimed to have encrusted the pair of shoes with a million-dollar diamond heart, which was lost during the brawl and never recovered.

The photo of the billionaire being handcuffed by the Meryton Police, his clothes in disarray, was featured by tabloids around the globe for several months. Today, he will serve his sentence at Ice Cream Vision, an organisation which produces and distributes free ice cream for poor children in the neighborhood.

The Meryton Weekly

***

"Now cut open the last ice cream tub lengthwise. What do you see?" asked the Quality Control manager of the day, whose name was Elizabeth.

Darcy did as he was told and replied, with a deadpan expression, "I see ice cream."

"It's Marble Fudge!" she said sternly. "The fudge should be evenly swirled throughout the container. If there is too much, or not enough, or if it is not properly distributed, then the product is rejected."

"Who would care about such a thing? Children get a Marble Fudge to eat, not to look at it."

"We care about our quality, Mr. Darcy!" She now had her hands on her hips. "So, what is your verdict?"

He lifted the carton up and took a quick glance. "Seems fine to me." Then he tossed it back onto the lab bench with a bang, accidentally knocking other cartons of ice cream around, splashing half-melted ice cream everywhere.

She jumped away, but some of the ice cream got onto her face and clothes. "That's no way to treat our beloved creations," she exclaimed, clearly annoyed. "Not to mention the mess you've made of the lab and of my clothes."

"I can help you clean up." He pushed her down to sit on the bench, then leaned over to lick a smear of vanilla from her nose.

She tried to shove him away, but he had his arms wrapped tightly around her.

"I'll report you to the authorities!" she cried.

"Report away," he murmured, and sucked a drop of chocolate ice cream from her earlobe.

A shiver ran through her body, and she braced her hands against his broad chest. "Mmm," she moaned, "I think I'll sell the story to the press instead."

He lowered his mouth to taste the strawberry ice cream on her smooth throat. "I can pay you far more to keep your mouth shut."

Her head dropped back as she chastised him. "I'll tell your wife that you played nooky at work."

"My wife is playing nooky with me now." Grinning, he parted her legs and positioned himself between them. Then he pulled down the neckline of her shirt, baring her gorgeous breasts. He used both hands to squeeze them hard, and said, "These cherry ice cream cones are in perfect shape. They will definitely pass my QC."

Capturing one hardened nipple between his teeth, he devoured the cherry, making her moan more loudly. Sticking out his tongue, he brushed it over her pink skin. Then his hands abandoned her bosom and headed south, busily unzipping his trousers and ripping off her panties.

"What kind of community service is this?" Elizabeth demanded weakly, slipping her hands into his trousers to grab his tight bottom. "Why should you get to enjoy your judicial punishment?"

He raised his hand and glanced quickly at his watch. "The official sentence ended fifteen minutes ago," he said, and lowered her to lie flat on the bench top. "Now the unofficial sentence and taste-testing begins." With that last word, he grabbed her hips and thrust his manhood into her hot entrance.

"Ah!" she screamed in delight. Her hands flew out to grasp the bench, upsetting more ice cream onto their bodies in the process. She felt his thick, rock-like shaft impale into her sensitive inner muscles again and again, scorching every pore in her passage, spreading the fire from her core down to her thighs and toes, and up to her belly and breasts.

"Yes!" she cried out as he continued to rapidly grind his shaft against her womb. His hands flew to her twin peaks, fondling and kneading them vigorously.

When he lowered his head and used his mouth to nip up a large mouthful of Marble Fudge and push the icy, creamy liquid between her lips, it tipped her over the edge.

The chilled fluid made the muscles inside her mouth tremble, resonating with the inner convulsions she experienced as she crested to her peak. Her legs wrapped tightly around his hips, sealing his cold belt buckle against the feverish muscles of her inner thigh.

As she arched her body up, he yelled out loud and spilled his burning seed into her.

Oh, what a tasting! Darcy wanted to try more flavors, preferably in a variety of positions. The thought made him hard immediately. Inspired, he withdrew his shaft from her warm entrance and turned her over.

A passion-weakened Elizabeth found that she was in for another amazing temperature treatment. Her naked breasts were now pressed against the cold lab bench, while her buttocks were pounded repeatedly by her husband's sweaty, burning body. Yet again, she was amazed by how he managed to last and last in order to bring her to peak after peak of pleasure.

***

The billionaire convict William Darcy was seen departing from Ice Cream Vision three hours after he was supposed to have finished his community services. He left the premises grinning, in the arms of his wife, Elizabeth Darcy, who was believed to be the local woman originally at the centre of that fight with Wickham. The Darcys married six months after the assault.

People demanded an investigation into Darcy's sentencing. They suspected that bribery was involved in having him assigned for community service at an organisation started up by his wife in Meryton. Will this odd job for the rich boy teach him to better control his anger in future? Only time will tell.

The Meryton Weekly

What if Mr. Darcy participated in a reality show?

SEXPERT CHALLENGE

"William, please? Please! Have I ever asked you for a favour?" Georgiana Darcy clung to her brother's arm, shaking it and pleading with him.

"Georgie, you ask me for favours every day." Darcy was busy reading a scientific report, and didn't look up at her.

Georgiana grabbed hold of his report, thrust it aside and said, "But this is my first job! Lady C is so kind to have given me the job of Production Assistant. This is her new quiz show. Please! What will you lose by agreeing to compete?"

"What kind of quiz show is it again? And the name?"

"I don't know the details yet. Lady C just asked me to find four celebrity participants who have a good general knowledge of life. She said they would be paired up with four 'normal' participants. The four pairs compete for half an hour for each of three episodes. The winners will get a prize. The losers will have a little bit of a joke played on them. It will be shown on Channel 12 next season at 9.30 pm on Tuesday nights. And the points you earn will be converted to cash and donated to the charity of your choice."

"Your aunt has produced a lot of rubbish, through the years, and Channel 12 generally broadcasts stupid shows. Can you imagine what my fellow researchers would say if they saw me on a stupid quiz show?"

"But you're helping charity – and your family! Lady C said she's had a difficult year, and I'm new in the business. If I do a good show, I might be invited to work on something bigger and better, like ' When the Maiden Meets the Prince'."

"I don't know why you're so obsessed with this show. You're rich and elegant, and you can have any European prince you care to name."

"But it's like pairing Cinderella with Prince Charming. I'll be the fairy godmother."

"Why you would want to be a fairy godmother is beyond me!" He sighed. "Who have you persuaded, so far?"

"I got Charles and Richard. I just need you and one more."

"Well, at least Charles and Richard will share in the embarrassment."

She beamed. "Thank you! Here's the contract. You can ask your lawyer to have a look, but once you sign it, no backing out, understood?"

"Just get out of my study now. I need to finish reading that report."

***

Lydia Bennet was badgering her sisters in much the same way, on the phone.

"Come on, Jane and Lizzy, you have to help me. This is my big break in TV, my first PA job. What's so difficult about being on a quiz show? You two are the intelligent ones."

"9.30 pm on Channel 12 is the doggy bit, Lydia. You know their shows aren't my kind of shows," Elizabeth said.

"But Lady C is reputable for serious productions. She made The Strongest Link and Sale of the Decade. Do you really think she would do anything too stupid? And she said she needed someone with good general knowledge about life."

"So?" Elizabeth was still uninterested.

"Jane, I heard from the other PA that Charles Bingley would be on the show."

"Oh, then we're lost!" Elizabeth exclaimed.

"Why did he agree to do it?" Jane asked. Jane had exchanged goo-goo eyes with Bingley throughout his stay at the Bennet Outback Resort in Boobie Hill, two months earlier. Things had been heating up when Bingley was suddenly called back to Sydney on business. They still kept in touch via email and phone, but they hadn't been able to see each other again since his departure.

"He is a family friend of Lady C, apparently. You don't want to miss a chance to get cozy with him again," Lydia said.

"How long will it be?" Jane asked.

"We'll be filming on a small island in Fiji. That's an additional incentive to compete. We'll stay there for a week. Imagine! A week on a romantic island with Charles Bingley. And the winners and participants will be given prizes, too."

"Does that mean that Darcy the Bighead will be there, too?" Elizabeth recalled her run-in with Darcy during his stay with Bingley. Darcy had met her at a party, where he had the audacity to say that she was 'only tolerable, not pretty enough to dance with.' For the remainder of his stay, Elizabeth had challenged his opinions at every opportunity, which was pretty often since Jane had liked to drag Elizabeth along when she first met up with Bingley.

Lydia replied, "Darcy? I don't know. He is a boring scientist with such a high IQ that he's sure to win if he competes. I don't think Lady C would want him on her show."

"Lizzy, please, do say you will go with me," Jane pleaded.

"You don't know any of the other participants?" Elizabeth asked.

Lydia crossed her fingers and said, "Not yet". *There's no need to tell Lizzy I've asked cousin Collins, too. She'll blow a gasket if she gets paired up with him.*

***

When the eight participants met at the plane to Fiji, there were some happy and some not-so-happy reunions.

Jane and Charles were so delighted to see each other, they practically jumped into each other's arms. They stuck together, ignoring everyone else, most of the time.

Darcy was furious with Georgiana for not telling him that Caroline the Climbing Ivy would be there, too. On the other hand, he was ecstatic to see Elizabeth the Little Hottie again. He'd had the hots for her ever since he stayed with Bingley at her family resort.

Elizabeth had half-expected Mr. Bighead, so she was not very surprised at seeing him, but she was livid with Lydia for inviting Collins the Sticky Gum. She was sure the week would be a torture, because Collins always imagined himself to be in love with her, and stuck to her, every chance he had. Her only consolation was that Charlotte, her best friend, was also there. The only contestant she didn't know was Richard Fitzwilliam. He seemed to be a friendly guy, so there might still be *some* joy left in the week.

***

They were each given a simple bungalow. *For just three episodes of TV, the production company sure spent a great sum of money*, Elizabeth thought.

After settling in, everyone gathered at the resort's ballroom, which had been turned into a TV studio with a lot of props and many people working.

Lady C announced, "Thank you for joining our show. Just a word of warning – anything you say or do in the studio will be filmed. We will use some of the more interesting bits as bloopers, so think before you say or do anything stupid here. But, of course, we won't be filming outside.

"Now, on to the details. You will be the first participants on our show. There will eventually be nine episodes, and you will compete in three of them. We will film here three times, with two different sets of participants after you folks.

"The format of our show is very simple. We pair you up into four groups, and then you answer some questions, play some games and do some role-playing. All of you will receive a small personal prize for participating, and your points will be converted into cash to be donated to a charity of your choice. The final winner of the third episode will win a prize of two nights at the next island. Before any of you say that you're too busy for the prize, I've asked our PAs to clear your calendar for two more nights, in case you win. The losers, however, will receive a 'torture'."

"Torture!" all of the participants exclaimed.

"Lydia, you didn't say anything about that!"

"Georgiana, I'm going to kill you!"

Lady C cleared her throat and said, when silence fell, "They didn't know. The format of the show was a secret. Anyway, it's not a real torture, just a trick, like dumping cold water on you, that sort of thing."

"Lady C, you never produced anything this stupid."

"Darcy, shut up. This is not stupid. This is entertainment. As you may remember, we asked you to fill out a form of what you like and dislike. We'll be making you face your fear. You, for instance, hate spiders, so we may put a spider on you if you lose."

People burst into laughter. *No Spiderman, our Mr. Bighead,* Elizabeth thought.

"Now, as to the pairings…"

Caroline waved her hand enthusiastically and said loudly, "I want to pair with Darcy!" Then Bill Collins moved near Elizabeth and yelled, "I'm here with my beautiful Lizzy."

"Be quiet! The pairings and your costumes were decided when you selected your drinks just now. We have assistants watching here, so no exchange is allowed. As you see, all of the men have blue cocktail glasses and the women all have red ones. Now, if all of you will take the stirrer out and bite off the cherry, you will see a number there."

"A penis-shaped stirrer! What sort of show are we on?"

"Shut up, Richard! Caroline Bingley, what is your number?"

"Four," she replied reluctantly.

"All right, 'four' is for a costume from Priscilla, Queen of the Desert."

"But, damn it, that's ugly! I won't dress in such ugly stuff."

"William Darcy?"

"Three," Darcy announced, and breathed a sigh of relief. *At least, I won't be paired up with the Climbing Ivy. It would be good to pair up with Little Hottie...*

"'Three' is for Batman and Catwoman."

"With the mask?"

"No, we want the audience to see your face. Jane Bennet, what is your number?"

"One."

"'One' is for the Indian costume. Richard Fitzwilliam, what have you drawn?"

"Two."

"'Two' is for ancient Greek costume."

"Charlotte Lucas?"

"I'm with Richard, I've two."

"Bill Collins?"

"Four. Can I change? I don't want to be with this hyper lady here. I want my Lizzy."

Good. Caroline and Bill deserve each other, Elizabeth thought. *But that means I'm either with Charles or ...*

"Charles Bingley?"

"I'm with this angel! I got one."

Yes! Darcy shouted in his mind, *Little Hottie is with me!*

"Show yours, Elizabeth Bennet!"

"I've three." Elizabeth turned to look at Darcy. She hadn't talked much with Mr. Bighead yet, but he had been staring at her during the whole trip to Fiji. *I hope he's as smart as he said. I don't want any torture.*

"I don't like the pairing. I'll quit if I'm not paired up with Darcy," Caroline said petulantly.

"Miss Bingley, I warn you. You have signed the contract, agreeing to participate in the show. If you quit now, I can sue you. However, since I can't allow any disruption to the filming, that is why I've security men and women here. For cases like this," Lady C said. "Annesley, take Miss Bingley to the Number Four changing room and see that she changes into the required costume."

"What are you doing? Let go of me!" Caroline was kicking and screaming. People couldn't hide their laughter when they saw her carried over the shoulder of a strong, heavy-set security woman.

***

"Georgiana, you never said I would be handcuffed to Elizabeth and strapped to the seat!" Darcy said. His left hand was tied to Elizabeth's right one.

"Lydia, why does this costume have so many seams? They seem to fall open at any time!"

"Quiet, everybody! Just be patient and all will be revealed. And now here's our host, George Wickham."

"Yuck! That slimy man."

"Oh, I think he's quite charming."

"His charm is all fake."

"Let's begin the show. If you all calm down and answer the questions, you can get out of your handcuffs and costumes much faster."

After a brief introduction, Wickham started the quiz.

"Name the location of one of the first two sperm banks in the world."

Buzz!

"Richard and Charlotte?"

"Tokyo."

"Correct. In which country did the oldest sex manual, *Handbooks of Sex*, originate?"

Buzz!

"Richard and Charlotte?"

"China."

"Correct."

"Hey Lady C, I thought this show was about general knowledge. Why are all of the questions about sex?"

"Cut! Darcy, you're wasting everyone's time. Isn't sex a part of life?"

"Yes, but I'm a serious scientist. I refuse to participate in such a stupid show."

"You can refuse to answer any question, but then you and your partner will lose and receive your torture in the end. It just shows your fellow scientists that you're less knowledgeable than your playboy cousin."

Richard groaned. "Now, Lady C, do you have to tell the world I'm a playboy? How can I chat up the pretty ladies here, if they know who I really am?" He flashed a grin.

"Shut up, Richard! Now that you know more about the show, we can tell you the name of it. Wickham!"

"Yes, my Lady. Welcome to Sexpert Challenge, a fun new show."

"What? Sexpert Challenge!"

"How can I face my colleagues when it comes on air?"

"Damn!"

"Lydia, I'm going to kill you!"

"Georgie, you will be dead, too!"

"Let's roll tape," Lady C shouted.

Wickham resumed his questioning of the contestants. "Who was the author of *Fanny Hill, Memoirs of a Woman of Pleasure?*"

Buzz!

"Darcy and Lizzy?"

"Henry Cleland."

"Correct. According to *The Sexual Anatomy of Woman* by W. F. Benedict, a girl of fourteen has breasts weighing how many kilograms – 5, 7 or 10?"

Buzz!

"Charles and Jane?"

"7 kilograms."

"Correct. Who was the actress who played *Deep Throat?*"

Buzz!

"Bill and Caroline?"

"Lindsey Lovelace."

"Wrong. The correct answer is Linda Lovelace."

"Fuck!"

"Cut! Caroline Bingley, mind your language. We can't broadcast foul language."

The quiz continued for several more minutes before Wickham announced, "We have now finished the first segment, 'Foreplay'. Let's recap. Richard and Charlotte are leading, at 70 points. Bill and Caroline are at the bottom with 50 points. Richard and Charlotte, you two get to choose the torture box for Bill and Caroline."

"Fuck! Let me go! I don't want to participate. I don't want any torture."

"Cut! Wickham just continue and ignore her. We will tape all her outbursts and show her worst moments later on the show."

"Fuck! You can't do that! I'll get my lawyer to sue you if you show me in any bad way on TV."

"My, my. I'm so afraid! Let's roll the tape."

Wickham cleared his throat. "Richard and Charlotte, which torture box would you like to inflict on them?"

"Charlotte, you choose."

"Such a gentleman," Wickham remarked.

"I hate Number 4, personally, So let's inflict Number 4 on them."

"Number 4? Let me see, it's… Ah, yes. Let's meet the cockroaches!"

The lighting in the room dimmed, and a spotlight shone on two cockroaches dangling down from the ceiling onto Bill and Caroline. Both of them screamed and tried to break away from their handcuffs or move off from their chairs.

But they were strapped securely in place, each with one hand cuffed to the partner. When the cockroaches were lowered onto their bodies, they both used their free hand to try to flick them away, but the strings attached to the cockroaches were very strong. The contestants' screams were deafeningly loud.

Luckily, the torture lasted for less than a minute. The strings were withdrawn, and the cockroaches ascended quickly toward the ceiling.

"Didn't either of you notice that those cockroaches were only plastic?" Wickham asked, flashing a devilish grin.

Everyone in the studio except for Bill and Caroline broke into chuckles.

"Fuck! That's not funny at all."

"And now for the second segment of our game, 'Arousal'. We have fitted each of you with a lie detector, and we will now ask you a question. If you answer truthfully, the light on the console in front of you will turn green, and a chime will sound. If you lie, the light will turn red, and something…interesting will drop down. Each one of you will be asked only one question. It's really very easy. And now for our first question.. Richard, have you ever had sex in your parent's bed?"

"No way!"

A rat dropped down onto Richard's head. He jumped and yelled loudly.

"Just a fake rat. But what a naughty boy! Testing out your parent's bed," Wickham said. "Now, Charlotte, it's your turn. Have you ever looked at men's underwear in a catalogue just to ogle the models?"

Charlotte hesitated before answering, "Yes."

Ding! The light turned green.

"Good girl! And with a healthy appetite! Now Bill, have you ever been to a strip club?"

"No, I'm a teacher. I've to uphold…"

A cup of cream was dumped onto him.

"Hey, the lie detector didn't work! I've never been to a strip club."

"Admit it, man! There is nothing wrong about going to a strip club. Now, Caroline, have you ever had a cosmetic surgery?"

"Of course not!"

A bag of honey was dumped onto her. She screamed and cursed about the mess.

"Famous model with fake body parts! I wonder which part you had done. How unfortunate that I can only ask one question! Now, Charles, have you ever taken part in a threesome?"

"No, that's gross."

Ding!

"What a straight guy! Now, Jane, have you ever gone to work wearing no panties?"

"No way. I'm not that kind of girl."

Ding!

"What an angel! Now, Darcy, have you ever fantasised about having sex with any of the women in this room?"

Darcy blushed. *Should I tell the truth?* "Yes."

Ding!

"Who's the lucky one?" Wickham asked.

Darcy only glared at Wickham.

William only knows me here. So he fancies me mad! I'll visit his bungalow tonight, Caroline thought with satisfaction.

"Now, Elizabeth, have you ever had sex on a plane?"

"A member of the 'mile high' club? No, I haven't had the privilege of joining it yet."

Ding!

"Let me tell you how to register as a member, after the show." Wickham winked at her.

Elizabeth smiled calmly, but Darcy wanted to punch his dirty mouth.

Then next round of the quiz continued. At the end of the first day of shooting, Darcy and Lizzy discovered that they had won. Bill and Caroline lost again, and were treated to the latest torture, as two bags of cold water were dropped onto their heads. That sent them into squeals, while everyone else laughed.

"The winners of the first episode, Darcy and Lizzy, will be rewarded with a treat. Which lucky pouch would you like?"

"Elizabeth, you choose."

"No, you answered most of the questions," she said to Darcy. "You choose."

"Hey now, Darcy and Lizzy, always so polite, how about I choose for you?" the flamboyant Richard offered, barging in.

Darcy glared at him and nudged Lizzy's arm.

"Number 3, please," Lizzy said.

"Lucky Pouch 3. Let me see… Ah! A full body massage with Fiji's miracle rocks."

"Good, I can use a massage," Elizabeth said.

The straps on the chairs were loosened for Darcy and Elizabeth, but they were still handcuffed to each other on one hand as they were led to their changing room.

"Hey, Lady C, why is the camera still rolling? I thought you said you wouldn't be filming us outside of the studio. And why are we still handcuffed together?"

"The treat is part of the show. Of course we'll be filming it. What is your problem? There is nothing objectionable about being filmed while you're given a massage."

Darcy glared at her, but she ignored him. The changing room was set up with a double bed behind a screen. Darcy and Elizabeth moved to sit on the bed.

"Annesley, help them take off the clothes," Lady C instructed.

"Hey, I don't need help. Just take off the handcuffs and I can do that myself," Elizabeth said.

"Miss Bennet, the handcuffs won't be taken off until we finish the day's filming. That is why we fitted you with costumes that have so many seams. It is much easier to tear them off. We won't film you naked, don't worry. The crew will stay behind the screen until you settle face down on the bed with towels covering your bottoms."

"Lady C, this is the dumbest thing you have ever done! How can you involve Georgiana and me in such a scheme? I don't want this so-called treat! I just want to go back to my room and rest."

"Shut up, Darcy. You have no choice. Annesley, move!"

The heavy woman came to tear off Darcy's costume first. He tried to fend her off but she was strong. After the leather top and trousers were torn away, she placed her hands on the waistband of his jockey shorts.

"Hey, I can get a massage with my underpants on!"

Rip!

The underpants were torn off, as well. Darcy flopped immediately onto the bed, face down, to hide his manhood, pulling Elizabeth down at the same time.

Elizabeth, who had observed him being stripped, was highly amused at first, and quietly amazed that he sported such six packs on his broad torso. She hadn't paid much attention to him after his arrogant remarks, but his thighs were strong and muscular. His whole body was a surprisingly healthy tan colour. She had expected him to be pale and sickly, as a nerdy scientist was supposed to be…but then, when she caught a glimpse of his manhood, she had swallowed hard. *One way or the other, it looks as if I gave him a most appropriate nickname. What a really BIG head! And his butt, so tight!*

She was concentrating too much on Darcy's body to notice that Annesley had moved on to her. The big woman tore off Elizabeth's leather top, exposing the red bikini bra underneath. To spare herself further embarrassment, Elizabeth laid face down beside Darcy and let Annesley remove the rest of her clothing from behind.

Darcy felt his arousal building when he saw her gorgeous breasts cupped in the red bikini top. Unfortunately, she laid face down when Annesley stripped her naked, so he didn't get to see more of her lovely breasts. But he couldn't keep himself from watching her taut creamy bottom. All too soon, their lower bodies were covered with towels.

Then the camera crew and the Fijian masseurs came in.

Elizabeth and Darcy were treated with fragrant oil and experienced hands that kneaded and rubbed. Then several hot rocks were placed on their backs.

Unconsciously, they turned their faces toward each other, peeking through half closed eyes at each other's naked flesh. Darcy's gaze focused on her creamy peak shaking against the bed while Elizabeth's eyes rested low on his body, taking in his tight butt under the towel. They each fantasized about what they wanted to do with the other's bodies.

Elizabeth tried to be stern with herself. *Remember, Mr. Bighead thought you were not pretty enough! What a pity! I wouldn't mind testing his big equipment. Truly, it's not a sin to lust after a condescending man…*

Darcy, too, was giving himself a lecture. *Remember, Little Hottie has a tacky family! What a pity! I wouldn't mind shagging her for days. Truly, it's not a crime to ache for an unsuitable woman...*

***

"Cut!"

It was a relief for Darcy and Elizabeth when the camera crew and the masseurs left the changing room. The massage was relaxing but the presence of others and the sexual tension between them was stressing.

In her hurry, Annesley dumped the key of the handcuff and Darcy and Elizabeth's normal clothes on the double bed, then left without releasing them.

When the door slammed shut, Darcy was the first to move. He moved to his knees on the bed, dislodging the small towel covering his butt.

Elizabeth eyes widened when she caught sight of his naked flesh again. When Annesley had removed his clothes earlier, she had already thought he was big, but he seemed to have grown even larger during the massage. *How can he have an arousal just from lying there? Was it the massage that aroused him, or me?*

She saw him searching among the clothes. Then she heard him moan and noticed that he had grabbed hold of her red lacy bra, instead of the key to the handcuff.

He dangled the intimate apparel in front of her eyes and said, "Very sexy!"

She turned to grab the bra from him, then realized that the move was a mistake, for she saw his eyes widen as his gaze zeroed in on her breasts and then moved lower to the dark triangle at the apex of her thighs.

Anxious to get away from his voracious gaze, Elizabeth tugged the bra harder, accidentally pulling Darcy off-balance and he tumbled down onto her half-turned body. She now had this big impressive man on top of her, with one of his hands linked to hers with a lacy bra and the other linked with a handcuff. His rigid arousal pressed against her hip, and his long legs tangled with hers.

The impact gave her an electric shock. She breathed deeply, trying to calm herself, but that made things even worse. The aroma of warm coconut oil and the musky scent from his body flooded her nostrils, and the expansion of her chest made her touch his more closely. His torso was smooth from the oil and the sweat. The pressure of the hard muscle instantly made her nipples peak.

They exchanged a hungry look, and then meshed their mouths together for a sizzling kiss. Their tongues duelled in rapid movements, and their hands hastily explored each other's bodies. Darcy hadn't let go of the lacy bra. He rubbed Elizabeth's body through it, giving the caress an additional dimension of sensation for both of them. He was extremely fond of her breasts. He weighed the creamy globes and rubbed the nipples with his fingers fervently.

With one hand restricted by the handcuff, Elizabeth moved her other hand to explore his back and taut butt cheeks, squeezing and sizing every bit of his big body.

In the course of the exploration, she settled on her back, with him fully on top. His hard shaft found its way between her thighs and teased her secret lips. She moaned out loud and nearly came in that instant. Then a voice broke through her ecstasy, and she heard him asking, "Elizabeth, are you safe?"

"Safe?"

"Yes, are you on pill? I've no condom."

"Damn! No!"

"Damn!"

They hugged each other tightly for a moment, and then broke away as if they had been scorched by fire.

Darcy rolled from her body and lay on his back.

Both of them took deep breaths.

After endless minutes, Elizabeth moved to find the key. She removed the handcuff and rose to put her clothes on with her back to him.

When she turned back to look at him, his eyes were closed and he was still breathing hard. He had pulled his shorts over to cover his manhood.

"You're okay?"

"Can we wait and talk after dinner?" He asked.

"I guess so."

"You go first. I still need a few more minutes."

With a last lingering look at him, she left the changing room.

***

When Elizabeth walked into the dining room, she felt awkward. It was one thing to lust after an arrogant man you didn't like, but to nearly have sex with him while handcuffed together was another; and they hadn't talked much since meeting again for the show.

I hope he won't think of me now as a loose and easy woman who jumps into bed with just anyone. Will he ask me to spend the night with him? Should I or shouldn't I?

With that troubling thought in mind, she put on her most serious and distant look when her gaze clashed with his across the dinner table. He was sitting there with a closed expression. Caroline was all over him on one side, and Richard on the other.

Elizabeth sat down in the only seat available, between Charlotte and Jane. They greeted her cheerfully and asked, "How was the massage? Did you enjoy it?"

She couldn't help but blush and murmured, "So so." She glanced at Darcy, not sure if he had heard their question.

Apparently so; she could see that he was blushing, too. To divert the group's attention, she asked in turn, "Where's Lydia? I want to chew her out royally for landing us all on this ridiculous show."

"Both your sister and Georgie are hiding from us," Richard said from across the table. "I was going to bite Georgie's head off when I next saw her; but then I thought, if not for her, I wouldn't have met all the lovely ladies from Boobie Hill."

"I can't imagine what sort of silly games they will have tomorrow. As a teacher, I feel that it's highly improper for me to engage in stupid games. If it weren't for my sweet Elizabeth, I wouldn't ..." Collins said.

"At least it will be good for the business. They mentioned the Bennet Outback Resort several times when they introduced Jane and Lizzy," Charlotte said, cutting off Collins when she saw that Elizabeth was embarrassed by his endearment.

"Darcy, you have to tell us – who's the lucky lady you fancy?" Richard asked.

Caroline, who had one hand on Darcy's shoulder and another on his arm, sat up straight. Seeing Darcy turned bright red, she came to his defence. "Mr. Playboy, it's none of your business who Darcy fancies."

"I see, Miss Ivy, that you don't delude yourself into thinking that Darcy fantasises about you."

"Miss Ivy? Delusion? What do you know about my relationship with William?"

"Isn't your nickname Climbing Ivy? I thought Dar... Ouch!" Richard yelped in pain. "Who kicked me?"

"I didn't know you were afraid of rats, Richard," Bingley said, diverting the attention from his sister.

"My torture was nothing. Imagine mixing honey, cockroaches and fake breasts together! It will make for the most interesting gossip when the show airs."

"Richard Fitzwilliam, if you say one more time that I've anything fake, I'll sue you!" Caroline swore.

"Aren't those fake eyelashes that you have there?" Everyone except Caroline broke out into chuckles. "Charles, can your sister sue me if what I said is true?"

"Leave her alone, Richard."

"But she barged into my conversation with my cousin, not the other way around. Now Darcy, fess up, who's the lady?" Richard elbowed Darcy and then suddenly snapped his fingers and said, "I know! Is it Lady C? Did you have a Mrs. Robinson fantasy about her when you were young?"

On hearing that outrageous speculation, Darcy choked on his wine and started to cough, glaring at his cousin.

Elizabeth burst out laughing. "Richard, you really are too funny!"

"Funny? Miss, I think you have no taste at all. Mr. Playboy's gross to imply that William might ever have such a thought." Caroline said.

"Oh, Caroline, relax! Richard is our resident comic relief. Darcy and I are used to him." Bingley said.

The banter and conversations continued, but no one was able to get a name from Darcy.

His plan to have a private conversation with Elizabeth was repeatedly foiled by Caroline, who kept close to his side all evening. When Elizabeth left to retire for the night, he thought about following her to her bungalow, but he still couldn't shake Caroline off. In the end, he only managed to escape when he went to Richard's room.

"How long will you be with Richard?" Caroline asked forlornly.

"A long time."

"I brought you a present from Paris. I want to give it to you tonight."

"Tomorrow's fine."

"What's your room number? I can wait there for you. Maybe you can give me your key."

Darcy shuddered and insisted, "Tomorrow." He then escaped into Richard's room and slammed the door shut.

***

Caroline was extremely vexed about the turn of events. She had thought she could force Darcy to reveal his fantasy tonight. She didn't mind giving the man a taste of her fabulous body. This would be a small step towards her grand plan to become Mrs. Darcy.

Why did he have to retreat to that blasted playboy's room? I wished I had paid more attention when they gave out room keys...

She was deep in her thoughts when she bumped into Annesley. "Hey, look where you're going, big lady!"

"Sorry, Miss Matchstick!" Annesley retorted.

Caroline was ready to put Annesley in her place...but then she saw that she was carrying a clipboard of papers.

"Is that logistics? I need to talk to William Darcy about something urgent. Can you check his room number for me?"

"I'm not supposed to give out that sort of info."

"Here's $20. Just check!"

Such a nasty woman! "Keep your money, Miss. Luckily for you, I'm in a nice mood tonight. William Darcy? Let me check... Ah. Room 12."

Caroline almost ran back to her room, forgetting the need to walk elegantly at all times. She decided to spend two hours to primp and perk her body up for the rendezvous with William. A facial, an orange-scented bath and a full-body oil treatment should do it. He was bound to be back to his room after two hours.

Knock or not? Better go through the balcony door. It's so hot tonight, I'm sure he'll have it open. And what a treat for him! Under the full moon, a perfectly toned body waiting to fulfill his every fantasy...

***

Caroline's seduction plan was working out as well as she could possibly have wished. Under her sensual silk wrap, she wore only an orange see-through negligee. She wasn't wearing a bra or panties. *Why hide the perfect body when I had paid so much for it?*

She was right on time, for once. And, to her immense satisfaction, she found the balcony door of Room 12 wide open.

But before she could sneak in to present herself as a present to Darcy, she heard a woman moaning loudly.

"So, you fantasised about me all those times? Why didn't you tell me earlier? No, don't touch it like that. Do it like this. Yes! Thrust harder. I haven't had an orgasm for decades…"

Caroline nearly fainted by the door! *How could you, William! With that ancient witch, Lady C!*

She crept on trembling legs off of the balcony, then ran back to her room as quickly as she could. After she slammed the door shut, she picked up the vase of flowers and threw it against the wall.

Her anger only subsided after she had smashed several other pieces of furniture in the room. Exhausted, she sat down on her bed. *Can I ever forgive his transgression? I didn't know he had a thing for old wrinkled woman.*

The practical side of her responded, *what's the difference? He's still loaded. You'll still have private jets, enormous yachts and all the designer clothes you want.* The thought of all the beautiful designer clothing finally calmed her down. *It's worth it!* She decided, then threw her tired body down on the soft mattress and went to sleep.

***

Outside the balcony of Room 12, a man sucked his cigarette hard, breathing in and out non-stop. It was his third consecutive one. He was unwilling to return to the bed. Such a demanding woman! Her skin was like sand paper! And her breasts sagged like hanging cucumbers! Such a lot of hard work, just for the position of a TV presenter! Damn!

***

Darcy was annoyed that he hadn't been able to find a moment all morning to talk to Elizabeth again. Everyone was gathered in the studio, as the shooting would start soon.

"Dear boys and girls, new costumes for a new day," Lady C said.

"What did she have for breakfast? She seems so cheerful this morning." Richard whispered to Darcy. The latter shrugged, but Caroline, who was standing right next to them, heard their exchange and shuddered.

"Do we get to change partners?" Collins asked.

"Sorry, my dear, no such luck. You're still stuck with Miss Supermodel. Now, all the gentlemen, please look under your coffee cups. There is a number written there. Richard, what number do you have?"

"Four."

"That is the cowboy and cowgirl costume. Collins?"

"One."

"That's the lion and leopard costume."

"Damn! Why do we always get the worst one," Caroline pouted.

"Bingley?"

"Three."

"That's the Pirates of the Caribbean costume. And that means that Darcy got two. That's the Regency costume. And now for our first game, 'Practise The Shot!'"

Two temporary horizontal bars were set up in the studio, spaced 2 metres apart. The female contestants were behind one bar, the men behind the other, with each pair of contestants facing each other across the divide. Each person had both hands handcuffed to the bar but spread slightly apart, and they were tied with a string at their waist.

Another string soon dropped down from the front. On the men's side, a banana was tied at the end of this vertical string, touching the ground. On the women's side, a tube 8 cm (around 3 inches) in diameter with openings on both ends was hung from the string.

"The game's really quite easy. Richard, Charles, Darcy and Bill, you just have to sway your body to swing the banana to hit the golf ball here into the tube of your partner. You'll score 10 points when the shot goes through. Of course, the lovely ladies on the other side can help to receive the balls by moving slightly to position the tube better for your shot. We'll have an assistant put the golf ball in the mark right in front of the men, and another assistant on the women's side to keep the score. So let's practise the shot!"

Elizabeth couldn't help laughing at Darcy. Gone was the nerdy scientist look. Also gone was the hot batman look. Along with his pristine tight shirt, waistcoat, trousers and riding boots, there hung a funny-looking small banana. He swayed his hips left, right, forward and backward, in every possible angle, but the golf balls just wouldn't cooperate. He sent some balls to Caroline's side, some to Jane's and one even as far as Charlotte's.

"Look at Bill! Use your feet to help," Elizabeth yelled to him.

"That's cheating!"

"They didn't say you couldn't use your feet. Quick! Or we'll lose."

Darcy followed her instruction and used his feet to help kick the banana to hit the balls. Finally, he put some through the target, but they still lost the round to Bill and Caroline.

"Bill and Caroline, which torture box do you want to inflict on them?"

"No, no torture for my sweet Elizabeth!" Collins said.

"Yes, no torture for William," Caroline added.

"Sorry, Bill and Caroline. We can't break the rules. Darcy and Elizabeth, how about you two choose a number?"

"Three," they said in unison, and looked at each other in surprise.

Wickham took out the note card from the torture box and said, "Oh, this is really no torture at all. Elizabeth, you just need to sit on Darcy's shoulders while he jogs around the studio three times."

"But I'm in Regency dress!" Elizabeth protested. "How can I sit on his shoulders?"

"Just hike it up. Do you want me to help?" Wickham asked, and winked.

"Let's not waste time. Annesley, help her mount Darcy." Lady C said, losing some of her cheerful countenance upon seeing Wickham's flirty manner toward Elizabeth.

Elizabeth was hot and flustered. To hike up her dress indecently in front of millions of TV viewers was embarrassing enough. But, to top it off, Darcy was grasping her naked thighs too tightly. Despite that, she didn't feel at all safe on her perch, because he was very tall. When he started to run, she felt as if she was sitting on top of a three-storey building, about to plunge to her death, so she bent her body lower and held tightly to his jaw, with her breasts practically resting on the top of his head.

In truth, Darcy had lost the game because he was so distracted by Elizabeth's low neckline. Her gorgeous breasts almost spilled out of the dress every time she laughed or bowed down to receive his balls. Now he was hyperventilating from holding her creamy thighs steady on his shoulders and feeling her secret lips rubbing the back of his neck. To make things worse, she bounced her breasts against the top of his head at every stride and held his throat tightly. He felt like he was going to be suffocated. He just hoped that no one would notice his bulge in the tight trousers of his costume, or suspect the true reason why he ran so awkwardly. *I may expire from the lack of oxygen, but my dead body will be fully aroused!*

When the torture run was finally finished, he was eternally grateful for Annesley's help in relieving him of Elizabeth, amid the chuckles of other people in the studio.

***

"Now for the second game: 'Fill The Bottle.' Blindfold the men, and then handcuff their hands behind their back!"

Once that was done, three special bottles were pinned onto various parts of the costume of each female contestant. The bottles were small and light, made of plastic so they didn't weigh down the costume. The pin was moulded onto the waist of the bottle, leaving the top open and easily accessible.

"Ladies, here are some marshmallows. Place one between your partner's teeth, then put your hands on top of your head and don't drop them at any time. We will deduct 5 points if you do so. You can tell your partner where the bottles are and instruct them to push the marshmallows down the bottle. Each bottle must have at least one piece of marshmallow. Each one will earn 10 points. Any extras he can push in will earn him 5 additional points. If your partner drops the marshmallow, our assistant will give you another one to place between his teeth. That is the only time that you're allowed to drop your hands from your head. Is that clear?"

"Bloody silly game!"

"So embarrassing!"

"I don't want to play!"

"Shut up, every one! Now spin the men around and lead them near their partners!"

When Darcy was led near Elizabeth, she said, "Open your mouth! Here's the marshmallow. I've one bottle near my right ni… chest, one near the… inside of my left thigh and one at the base of my spine. Which one do you want to try first?"

On hearing the locations of the bottles, Darcy eyes widened under the blindfold and he swallowed hard, accidentally gobbling the marshmallow down his throat.

"What did you gulp it down for? We're losing precious time!"

"Sorry, give me another one quickly. Let's start with your breast, uhm, chest." He could feel blood cruising down his body. Sweat broke out on his forehead.

Elizabeth put another marshmallow between his teeth, then moved nearer. When his chest touched her body, he started crouching down a bit, as he was taller than her. First, his jaw touched her right shoulder. Then he went lower and traced his way farther down her body.

Soon, his jaw felt her nipple. *So hard and firm! How I want to nibble on it! Don't think of that. You will disgrace yourself in front of everyone.* He was about to swallow again, but he remembered the marshmallow, so he stopped. Right underneath the nipple, he could feel the bottle.

To find the bottle opening, however, he had to lower his face onto her breast. He breathed in the scent of lavender; then, through the fabric, his nose grazed the hard tip of her nipple. He could feel his arousal cresting, and he froze.

"Drop it in!"

Elizabeth's breathless words startled him from his sensual trance. He shuddered, mouth gaping slightly open, and dropped the marshmallow onto the floor.

"Not again!"

Without waiting for him to recover, Elizabeth grabbed another piece from the assistant and placed it between his teeth. He still had his mouth near her nipple. "Quick! Push it into the bottle."

Darcy obeyed, but the bottle opening had been specially made to be slightly smaller than the size of the marshmallow. He couldn't just drop it in. Instead, he had to stick his tongue out and thrust the marshmallow into the opening.

As the bottle was dangling below her nipple, and her partner's head was bowed there, Elizabeth couldn't see whether he was successful. But she could feel the breath from his nose, blowing hot air onto her nipple. She then felt his mouth pushing down against the bottle, putting weight on her costume and stimulating her sensitive tip. She could also feel his tongue sticking out, grazing her peak as he thrust the marshmallow into the bottle. She could sense the heat gathering at her legs, making them trembled. She nearly dropped her hands from her head, because her whole body seemed to be on fire.

"Finally!" he said after pushing one in.

"Now, down to the bottle pinned on the inside of my left thigh," Elizabeth said weakly and placed another marshmallow between his teeth.

Darcy crouched farther down. His nose and mouth traced from her right nipple diagonally down to her left thigh, leaving a hot path across her body.

The bottle was pinned to Elizabeth's body in a most naughty way. Both the front and back panel of the dress were pinned together with the bottle, making the dress look like trousers. The bottle was hung about 10 cm underneath her womanhood, on the inside of her left thigh. She therefore had to stand with her legs wide open to allow Darcy's head to move into position there. She could feel her panties growing wet as she sensed Darcy's nose and mouth near her sex.

Darcy was not doing much better. He breathed in her womanly scent, and he could feel the heat of her body rising through the fabric of her dress. The bottle was so close to her apex that he practically had to touch her there, in order to reach the opening of the bottle. After attempting several angles, he finally managed to stick the marshmallow into the opening.

Thrusting it down into the bottle itself posed more of a challenge. His tongue seemed to have developed a will of its own. It wanted to thrust upward toward her hot entrance, instead of down to the bottle. In the end, the tongue won over the mind, sliding over the fabric and across her secret entrance. He could imagine her lips separating under the relentless pressure of his tongue...

"What are you doing?" Elizabeth was shocked by his move and backed away, which sent him stumbling to sit on the ground. As if in slow motion, Elizabeth saw the marshmallow drop down from the opening of the bottle onto the ground.

"Damn! We'll have to start all over again."

Luckily, other contestants were not doing very well, either. At the end of the game, it was the team of Charles and Jane that lost the round, as Charles had been so distracted by Jane's body that he'd dropped most of the marshmallows anywhere except inside the bottle. They were then treated to a torture: he had to do 20 push-ups with Jane riding on his back.

Another silly game was played, to conclude the second day of shooting. At the end of the day, Bill and Caroline won and were granted a mud spa. Charles and Jane lost and were treated to their final torture, with Charles jumping rope with Jane riding on his front – this time until they reached 50 jumps non-stop. Charles had no complaint, as he enjoyed shaking with Jane very much.

***

When Darcy entered the dining room, he was relieved to see that Caroline was not there. He gave Elizabeth a hot gaze. She was sitting with Jane and Charlotte again.

Richard greeted him. "Darcy, did you hear about Caroline?"

"What about her?"

"She had an accident in the mud spa, and the production company is taking her back to the mainland for emergency treatment."

"I hope it's not serious. Bingley, didn't you want to go with her?"

"No, apparently she just needs the attentions of a plastic surgeon for a few hours."

"A plastic surgeon?"

"Yes, it seems that one of her false body parts couldn't stand the heat in the mud spa." Richard winked and burst out laughing, "Sorry, Bingley. No offence to your sister, but I never knew fake breasts were so delicate. My medical knowledge seems to be seriously lacking. It's just that I can imagine your response on seeing her with two different sizes." With that, he turned aside to talk to Collins.

Most of the people around the table tried not to laugh, but they all had silly grins on their faces, even Bingley. The dinner atmosphere was much better without Caroline there, except for the constant fawning of Collins over Elizabeth.

When the dinner was finished, Darcy thought he might be doomed to another wasted day with no chance to talk to Elizabeth. Charlotte seemed to prefer talking to Collins more than Richard, tonight. She distracted Collins to the pool area but, unfortunately, Richard had Elizabeth's attention. Darcy, however, was not going to give up so easily, so he followed them toward the beach.

He was jealous of the easy manner in which they joked, teased and chatted. *Why is it that she does nothing but challenge me, when we were together? We never converse comfortably. Damn Richard! Always chatting up pretty girls and leaving them!* His mood became darker and darker as they progressed further down the beach.

When Richard playfully splashed some water on Elizabeth, dampening her sundress and making her squeal and retaliate, Darcy found that he had had enough. After several frustrating days, seeing Richard flirting with his Elizabeth was simply too much. He grunted a good night and stormed off to his bungalow, refusing to become a third wheel

He took another cold shower, to cool down all his violent thoughts about Elizabeth and Richard, but instead found himself recalling the scenes of the past two days, just Elizabeth and him alone, he with all the liberty in the world to kiss, bite, lick and fondle her naked body.

Not surprisingly, the cold shower didn't do much to lessen his arousal. He stalked out of the bathroom in a foul temper, naked and erect, only to come face-to-face with Elizabeth, who was tapping on the open balcony door and already had one foot in his room.

Elizabeth's eyes widened like saucers upon seeing his raging asset. She opened her mouth and stuttered, "You... You said... you... wanted to talk, but you ran... off so suddenly from Richard and me...and so I...I..."

On hearing Richard's name, Darcy's violent emotions returned in full force. He pulled Elizabeth into the room, slammed the door shut, and pressed her against the glass with a scorching kiss. His tongue invaded her mouth, pushing in and out, imitating the action he longed to apply her other entrance.

Elizabeth was unprepared for his violent reaction, but her body welcomed his rough ministrations. She wrapped her arms around his neck and used her tongue to play aggressively with his.

His hands tore open her damp, front-opening sundress, sending buttons flying. He then flipped open her bra, the better to fondle her twin peaks. Matching the thrusting rhythm of his tongue, his hands squeezed both of her breasts, hard and then softly.

Darcy was on fire. Kneeling, he pushed down her panties impatiently and threw them over his shoulder. Then his hands moved to worship her sex, pleasuring and wetting her. After a few minutes of rubbing, he could feel that she was ready for him. He rose and pulled her legs up to wrap them around his waist; then he lodged his huge manhood against her entrance and flexed his hips.

Despite her highly aroused state, she was very tight. He could only thrust into her a short ways before he had to slow down his tempo. He moved his hands to rub her breasts and folds, hoping the fondling would relax her.

Elizabeth moved her hands to rest on his shoulders and raised her body higher. Her legs also moved higher on his waist. Thanks to this new position, or to his continuous ministrations, or both, Darcy was able to push his thick shaft into her further. Her muscles engulfed him, giving him the greatest of pleasure. With one further mighty thrust, he drove himself right to the hilt. He could see her eyes roll back, and she let out a loud moan. Her fingers dug into his shoulders, and her legs squeezed his waist.

He moved his hands to her creamy bottom. Urged on by her dreamy expression, he started to thrust in and out, faster and faster. The hard thumping sound against the glass balcony door matched their loud moans.

After endless minutes of such frenzied mating, Elizabeth screamed out upon reaching her peak. Darcy thrust in and out a few more times before surrendering to the beguiling demands of her contracting inner muscles and spilling himself into her. The pulsing and orgasm lasted for a long, exquisite time.

When Darcy finally calmed down a bit, he moved away from the balcony door and collapsed onto the bed, carrying Elizabeth with him still. He then arranged her on top on him. She bent at her slender waist, pressing her breasts to his chest as he caressed her hair and back.

"Was I too rough?" he whispered to her ears.

"Wow! That was absolutely out of this world."

"Yes, for me too. I've never had such a great climax in my whole life."

The rough coupling and the sexual tension of the past two days had exhausted them both, and they soon drifted off to sleep.

Several times during the night, they awoke and pushed each other to more orgasms, more slowly and sweetly.

Near dawn, after they had savored another satisfying session of love making, Darcy said, "We didn't used a condom the first time. I've never done that in my life. I've never slept with a woman without protection."

"You were like an animal that had been starved for too long. And I haven't chewed you out royally, yet, for licking me during the marshmallow game. What if they caught you on camera?"

"I couldn't help it. They put on such naughty games, and I've had the hots for you for some time." He shook his head in wonder. "Tonight is a record for me – six trips to heaven."

"You're lucky it was me. I don't think Caroline's fake body parts could withstand your continuous heat and pressure," she said, and winked.

Darcy laughed out loud.

Elizabeth beamed. "You should laugh more often. You have dimples, and they make you look absolutely adorable."

"Seriously, though...is it a likely time of the month for you to get pregnant?"

"I don't know. I've never been that good at keeping track of such things. I want you to know that you're quite the exception; I've never slept with a guy I wasn't in a relationship with. In fact, you're only the third chap I've ever slept with."

"I know you don't sleep around. You're not the type. And you're so wonderfully tight. I was the irresponsible one here, making love with you without protection. I've been on fire for you ever since I stayed at your family resort, two months ago."

Elizabeth raised her head in surprise. "But you said I was only tolerable, and not pretty enough to dance with!"

Darcy groaned and apologized. "I was being pigheaded then, because I didn't want to go to Boobie Hill. I was very busy at that time, but all my friends and family said I had buried myself in my research for far too long, and they kicked me off to take the holiday with Bingley. I hadn't even looked at you clearly when I made that snide remark. Not long after that, I found you amazingly attractive, smart, caring, funny..."

"Hey, no need for all the flowery words. You've already gotten into my pants."

"So, would you move to Sydney with me, after we finish shooting here?"

"Move to Sydney! You're moving way too fast. I found you condescending, only a few days ago..."

"What? How could you sleep with me if you didn't even like me? I thought..."

"I told you that you were an exception. I guess I started lusted after you when I saw your big…asset during the massage. I couldn't help myself, even if you *had* looked down on all of us when you were at our Resort."

"Your mother was money-grabbing. She pushed Jane and Lydia shamelessly at Bingley and me. And your three younger sisters were trashy. Of course, you and Jane are totally different. To be honest about it, I never wanted to be associated with a tacky family…but I would be, for you."

Elizabeth stared at him, furious. Then she left the bed and pulled her clothes on quickly. Legs apart, hands on hips, she snapped, "You're the most arrogant and conceited man I've ever had the misfortune to meet and sleep with. No one can choose their family. I know my mother and sisters are loud and trashy, but I love them just the same. Do you mean to forbid me from seeing my family if I move to Sydney with you? Do you think all the money in the world could induce me to abandon them? Dream on! If you don't like my tacky family, you had better pray that you didn't make me pregnant. Otherwise, young Master High-and-Mighty Darcy Junior will have tacky origins, too."

"Elizabeth, you mistook me. I'm not good at words…"

Darcy sprang up from the bed and tried to detain her, but she shook him off and stormed out of his room with a loud bang on the balcony door.

He sank down onto the bed, held his head in his hands, and groaned. *Stupid man! Why did you have to put your foot in your mouth? Admit that you will willingly house 10 of her trashy family members if you can have her as your girlfriend. Clearly, neither your money nor your bedside manner move her. She only bedded you because she wanted to test your equipment. No love lost there. She loves her family with a passion, and you just trampled them into the ground. And she may be carrying your little junior. Damn. Damn!*

***

Caroline was gone for a day. Luckily, the shooting could afford to stop for a day, as the production team needed to work on the props for Episode 3.

She came back in the foulest mood. Her quick trip to the mainland to salvage the right implant had only been marginally successful. Now her breasts were slightly unbalanced, to her critical eye.

She also came back to find Darcy in a terrible mood. He wouldn't talk with anyone, except to growl or frown. And, of course, she couldn't put her seduction plan into action that night, as the new breast might not survive another puncture.

By the time the next morning came, she was numbered among the people who were in a dreadful mood.

***

Darcy and Elizabeth's tempers were shocking. He desperately wanted to explain his affection to her and plead with her again to come live with him. She was severe with herself for sleeping with Mr. Bighead without protection and then enjoying his lovemaking again and again throughout the night.

Her frame of mind darkened when she was shoveled into a big hotel suite with Darcy and a few assistants. She was then helped into a sexy French maid outfit while he donned a normal business suit with a waistcoat. She knew the role-play would be ghastly! She needed to get her hands on Lydia so that she could kill her.

The costume featured a flame-red corseted short skirt and a deep v-neck, black lace accents along the hem, trim and detailed side-lacing, garters, back zipper, ruffled lace panties, black ruffled lace sleeve bands with a red bow accent, black thigh-high fishnet stockings, white lace cap and white apron, a black feather duster and a pair of 4-inch high heels.

The assistant told them that the day's challenge would be shot individually, inside several suites. An hour before their session, the assistants would come back to set up the lighting and explained the rules to them. For the time being, however, they would leave, locking them into the suite to relax.

Elizabeth rolled her eyes. *How can I relax in this sexy French-maid gear, with a big bed and Mr. Bighead within arm's reach?*

Once the assistants were gone, Darcy took Elizabeth's hands, knelt in front of her and said, "Elizabeth, I'm sorry. I shouldn't have spoken about your family like that. I'm …awkward with strangers and I'm… socially inept. That's why Georgiana, Richard and Bingley always push me into big social functions, in the hope it will smooth out my rough edges. I I…like you a lot. I want to spend more time with you. I'll try my best to get to know your family. Will you give me another chance? I can take a few days off, after the shooting. May I come and stay with you? Then we could get to know each other a bit better."

Elizabeth wanted to shake him off, at first. But since he was apologizing, she let him continue. He did look sincere in his apology, and the fact that he was willing to come back to stay with her family again won him a huge brownie point. *Is he worth the time?* She looked him in the eye, and saw his anxiety and eagerness. *Of course, he is smart and handsome. He's nice to his friends and family. He just didn't smile and didn't talk with other people enough. And he's so damn hot in bed!*

"All right," she conceded, "you may consider yourself to be on parole here. But one wrong move and I'll send you packing."

Darcy was so happy that he hugged her tightly and gave her the silliest grin. "And if I behave well, you will think about moving to Sydney with me soon? I'll never forbid your family coming or you visiting them."

"It's way too early to think about that. Let's see how we go for a few months before we talk about moving in together."

Her reply put a dent in his happiness, but he reasoned that it was still a big step better than the day before.

He tried not to look at her, as she was so damn sexy in the French maid costume. They held hands and chatted comfortably for about an hour, until the production crew came in again.

"All right, we're ready for you now. This is a role-play where we won't give you any script. You two will walk into this set and we'll have an actor here to play along with you. Denny here has a script about a scenario and he will prompt you on, but we won't tell you what the scenario is until you walk in. If you find the role-play too silly and don't say a word, you will lose the game and end up with a torture. The wittier and cheekier your role-play, the more points you will earn. We won't ask you to do anything indecent. After all, we're bound for free-to-air TV. We will show everyone's role-play tomorrow. You can vote for your favourite one then. We have also invited some other people to judge the role-plays. All the scores will be added together to decide the winner. In the event of a tie, another role-play will be shot.

"Ok, ready? Let's roll the camera for episode 3 with Darcy and Elizabeth."

When Darcy and Elizabeth walked onto the set, Denny came forward, shook their hands and said, "Good that you're here, Darcy and Elizabeth!"

"Thanks," they replied.

"Okay, you two sit on the bed. Let me look at your CVs." Denny then sat on one of the chairs, a bit farther from the bed, "Husband and wife porn stars! How many porn movies have you two made together?"

Both Darcy and Elizabeth were speechless. They looked at each other. What kind of role-play was this?

Elizabeth recovered first and said, "Umh…Six. We've made six movies together."

"Great! Tell me your six favourite positions then. I mean privately, not in the movies. You still shag each other privately, I suppose?" Denny winked.

Darcy was still speechless, so Elizabeth replied, "Oh, the other …night we had the …traditional missionary position, doggie style …woman on top …standing up, on the side and 69 position." She turned bright red, thinking back to what they had done, the other night.

"Wow, you two sure know how to practise. So, Darcy, which parts of Elizabeth's body do you like most?" Denny was scripted to get responses from both participants, and so he directed the question to him.

"Umh…the chest. Definitely her chest," Darcy said, glancing sideways at Elizabeth's barely contained breasts in the corset.

"What do you like about her breasts?"

"Umh…very firm…and soft to sq…touch."

"Are they good to suckle?"

Darcy turned bright red and wanted to explode. *Silly game! I'm going to kill Georgie!* "Yeah," he replied in a barely heard voice.

"Sorry, I couldn't hear you. Do you like to suckle Elizabeth's breasts?"

"Yes!"

"And what do they taste like?"

Darcy wanted to smash Denny's head. He replied reluctantly, "Strawberry."

"I can see a good glimpse of her breasts here, but not the strawberries. What a pity!" Denny joked and received a glare from Darcy.

"So, this is a production about a French aristocrat taking advantage of his maid. Darcy, you stated on your CV that you speak French. Use the formal tense, as you're the master. Can you give me a few dirty lines?"

"Umh…Ouvrez vos pattes."

"Open your legs!" Denny translated. He must have been selected to host the role-play because he could speak French. "Good. A few more?"

"Repliez sur la table."

"Bend over the table! Excellent! How about 'You have big tits'?"

"Il y a du monde au balcon."

"Cool. Now, Elizabeth, it says here that you don't speak French, right?'

"Correct."

"Pas de problème. No problem. Here is the script for the screen test."

"Cut! Okay, we'll give you 10 minutes to read the script. You don't need to memorize it as actors are allowed to hold scripts when they do a screen test. When you're supposed to carry out an action – for instance, if there is kissing involved – you don't actually need to kiss if you don't want to, I suppose, but for a real-life screen test, of course, a real kiss would be needed. We know you're just participants on this game show, so you may not be comfortable with all of the acts written there," the producer said.

As Darcy and Elizabeth read the script, their faces grew redder and redder.

***

The next day, Darcy was sitting next to Elizabeth, holding her hand under the table. They had spent another steamy night together after their role-play. Now they were gathered with the others at the resort's ballroom to look at and vote for the clips from the role-plays. Besides the eight participants, some TV crew members had also been asked to be part of the judging panel.

Lady C said, "As you'll recall, those participants who didn't have a script for their segments were prompted by our hosts. Even when we gave the participants scripts, some didn't follow them. There is a score sheet in front of you. Please rate their performances according to how witty, sexy, funny, and entertaining you find the role-plays. First up are Caroline and Collins. Their role-play is entitled 'Collins Collins Pumpkin Eater.'"

When the film rolled, the audience could see Caroline, wearing a sexy orange bikini, kicking and screaming as she was placed inside a large, semi-transparent orange pumpkin shell. Collins stood to one side, wearing a farmer's costume. The host for the segment was Wickham.

"Farmer Collins, I'm Reporter Wickham from Agricultural Australia Monthly. I see you have grown a special pumpkin for this year's Agricultural Show. Indeed, you appear to have made your wife into a pumpkin. Why did you do that?"

"She likes to wander.... . She shags with Richard there all the time," Collins said stiffly.

"What? Why would he mention me there?" Richard protested. "Is he reciting from a script?"

The film rolled on. "What sort of fertilizer do you use to make her grow?" Wickham asked Collins.

"Well...mmm...dog shit, cow manure, mmh...food scraps... You know. The normal sorts of fertilizer," Collins continued.

"How does she react to such rich fertilizer?"

"She loves it. She has to have it twice a day, every day of the week."

"No wonder she has grown to such a size. We have some cow manure here. Can you show us how to apply it?"

Wickham handed Collins some dark-looking stuff, which the latter splashed and dumped onto Caroline.

"Stop it! Stop it! This is gross!" Caroline screamed. She was definitely not following a script. Her head and face were marred with the dark-hued shit.

"Miss Pumpkin Caroline, what's so gross about it?" Wickham asked.

"Get this yucky stuff off of me! Why do I've to partner up with this toad? Why can't I've a nicer outfit? I'll sue your pants off, bloody Lady C!"

Lady C interrupted the film and said to the group, "Don't worry about that last bit. It will be cut out."

"Interesting! Farmer Collins, your pumpkin can talk back. She called you a toad. Should you do something about her?"

"Yes. This pumpkin is...very annoying. It doesn't know how to stop talking. Let me try rolling and spinning her around." Collins proceeded to rotate the pumpkin with Caroline trapped inside.

"Stop, you toad! I'm going to throw up!" she screamed.

"Farmer Collins, I've heard that, despite your constant arguments with Miss Pumpkin Caroline, you're in fact very fond of her. Some neighbours tell me that you love your unfaithful wife very much. They saw you pampering her. Can you show us how you do that?"

Wickham handed Collins a broom, which Collins used to brush Caroline from head to toe, mashing the fake manure all over her face. Then a bucket of water and a toilet brush were handed to him. He proceeded to pour the water all over her and brush her down.

"I'm going to kill you…" she threatened shrilly.

Their role-play continued for a few more minutes. At the end, Collins peeled off Caroline's bulky pumpkin shell to reveal her sexy orange bikini once again. He attempted to give her a few kisses and fondle her a bit, to make the whole role-play sexy, but Caroline was furious. She grabbed the broom and toilet brush and chased Collins around, smashing his head with them.

Nearly all of the people in the studio watching the clip were laughing their heads off. Caroline and Collins were neither looking at nor talking to each other.

Lady C cleared her throat. "Now Charles and Jane, as Wild Tarzan and Jane. The host for this segment is Denny."

The couple were both in sexy animal costumes. Against a jungle backdrop, Jane appeared to be unconscious. Denny, in an ape costume, pointed to Jane's body and asked, "Tarzan/Charles, what do we have here?"

"An angel…? No, something like me," Charles replied.

"Not very alike."

"How so?"

"This one has two balls here and you don't." The 'ape' pointed from Jane's breasts to Charles's chest and said, "Squeeze them and tell me what they are like."

Charles's eyes widened. "Squeeze her breasts in front of …?"

"Why do you call them 'breasts'?"

"I… heard some other apes say it," Charles improvised.

"Squeeze!" the ape said, and elbowed Charles.

Charles knelt down near Jane and cupped her breasts lightly, making her moan.

"Oh, it moves. How did the round balls feel? Are they as hard as coconuts?" the ape asked.

"Of course not. They are firm but soft to touch."

"It seemed to have trouble breathing. You should give it some air." He elbowed Charles again.

"How?"

Ape/Denny grabbed Charles, kissed him on the mouth, and said, "Like that. Or do you want me to give her air?"

Charles pushed the ape away and bent over Jane to give her a soft kiss on the mouth. She gasped and her eyes opened.

"Well done, Tarzan/Charles." The ape poked Jane's shoulder. "What's your name?"

"Jane."

"How did you find Tarzan's mouth?"

"He's …soft. Quite nice."

"And how did you feel when he squeezed your breasts?"

"Mmm…nice."

"Tarzan/Charles, look under her animal-skin skirt and see if she is different below, too," the ape suggested.

"What? No way!" Charles and Jane protested.

"I'll look, then, if you don't." The ape moved, but Charles stepped protectively between the ape and Jane.

"Oh, you two are so boring!" The ape threw a tantrum. "Entertain me!"

"Why should we? I'm Tarzan. I should be the one commanding in the jungle."

"So you want me to entertain you with Jane here?" Ape pretended to chase Jane. She squealed.

Charles turned, picked her up and ran. Jane wrapped her arms around his neck and her legs around his waist.

The role-play neared a close with the ape chasing them into the jungle, through slippery foam. After a few slips and falls, both Tarzan and Jane, soaking wet, looked very sexy. Their performance also made many people in the studio laugh out loud.

"Next we have Richard and Charlotte as Crazy Cop and Innocent Housewife. Their host is Wickham."

"Officer Richard, who have you got there?" Wickham asked Richard. They were in a holding-cell setting.

"A housewife named Charlotte. A neighbour complained that a ring was missing, and she was caught lurking in the vicinity."

"Okay, Charlotte, hands on the wall, legs apart. Officer Richard, search her."

Richard obeyed and patting his way quickly down Charlotte's body, touching her only in inoffensive places.

"Hey, what did they teach you at the Academy? Search the lady thoroughly – or do you want me to take over? What do you say, lady? Which one of us do you want?"

"Not you. Officer Richard, please!"

"Move your butt, Officer."

Richard moved closer and ran his hands first over her arms, then moved towards her breasts.

"It's a ring we're talking about, Officer. You need to conduct this search slowly and thoroughly!" Wickham barked.

Richard slowed his tempo and moved his hands to cover her breasts. Both Richard and Charlotte were clearly flustered.

"Anything, Officer?"

"No, nothing."

"What? She doesn't have any breasts?"

"Sir, she doesn't have any ring hidden there."

"Okay then, move down to her other hiding space, Officer Richard."

Richard's breathing became quick and shallow. He moved his hands down her belly and then to the triangle at the apex of her legs.

"Found anything?"

"Nothing."

"Turn her around and tie her to the bars, wrists and ankles apart."

"What are you doing? Are you crazy?" Charlotte yelped.

"Now, you tell Officer Richard where you hid the ring or he'll have to use his top-grade interrogation technique."

"I want a lawyer! You can't do this to me!" Charlotte screamed.

Wickham handed Richard a gun, "Housewife Charlotte, this is a water gun. Fess up. Where is the ring?"

Charlotte yelled and called Wickham all sorts of names.

"Aim at her mouth to shut her up."

Richard did as was told.

"Damn, Richard, do you have to be so obedient?" Charlotte was blazingly angry now.

Richard grinned. "Sorry, he's the boss."

"Now, let's see what you learned about shooting at the Academy. As you can see, her white sundress has three red circles. Use them as your targets."

The audience's attention was drawn to Charlotte's white costume, which sported three red spots, each roughly 5 cm in diameter, placed 5 cm above her three most important areas.

Richard aimed and shot at the first circle above Charlotte's right breast. As the water touched the fabric, the material started to dissolve.

"Damn! They're made of rice paper!" Charlotte said.

His on-target shot left a 5-cm hole above her right nipple, allowing the audience to catch a glimpse of the flesh there.

"You're crazy! Who thought of such a thing?" Charlotte yelled.

"Officer Richard, the suspect accuses you of being crazy. Show her your crazy water gun."

Richard seemed to enjoy Charlotte's outburst. For the past few days of their pairing, he hadn't seen her lose her calm once. Privately, he thought that she looked rather magnificent when she was angry.

With a devilish grin, he proceeded to shoot water at the circles above her left breast and above the apex of her thighs, exposing two more erotic holes, revealing tantalizing glimpses of Charlotte's body for the audience to see.

The role-play ended when Richard was ordered to kiss and fondle his captive into submission. Their role-play earned a lot of applause and whistles from the audience. Charlotte blushed red, while Richard's face wore a silly grin.

"And now for Darcy and Elizabeth, our Husband and Wife Porn Stars Team. Denny's the host."

The film rolled to show the initial interview of Darcy and Elizabeth, applying for roles in a porn movie.

"This porn is about a French aristocrat taking advantage of his maid. Now action!" Denny continued.

Elizabeth, in her sexy French maid's gear, carried a tray of hot chocolate into the bedroom setting, prepared to serve her master, who had just come back from a business meeting.

"Monsieur, your hot chocolate," Elizabeth said.

"Put it on the bedside table."

"Darcy, you need to put some French accent in your line," Denny added.

"Put it on the bedside table." Darcy repeated with a heavy French accent.

When Elizabeth bent to place the drink down there, her ruffled lace panties were visible under the short skirt. Darcy moved behind her to trap her near the bedside table.

"Monsieur!"

He took the mug and drank a mouthful.

Denny came to stand beside them. Taking Darcy's hand, he placed it on Elizabeth's right butt cheek. "Pinch and continue."

Darcy pinched her bottom slightly.

"Monsieur, what are you doing?" Elizabeth whirled to face Darcy.

"The chocolate is not hot enough. I … want something… hotter."

"What do you mean, Sir?"

"The next action sequence is Darcy pushing you onto the bed. He parts your legs, smells your *chatte* – that's your pussy, in French – uses the feather duster to play with you, and then mounts you. Both of you must act to give me the best fake climax you can. This is a screen test. If you two want the roles in our production, you have to give me the loudest moans you can manage. Now action!"

When Darcy appeared reluctant, Denny elbowed him, urging him to move.

Darcy leaned toward Elizabeth, making her topple onto the bed. The action made her body bounce on the mattress, her breasts shaking enticingly under the corset. He bent down and parted her legs slightly, but he still seemed reluctant to bend down and smell her womanhood in front of the camera.

"Hey, man, do you know how to act? If not, move aside and I can show you!" Denny came forward and put a hand on Elizabeth's leg.

That alarmed Darcy. He exclaimed, "Don't touch her," then bent down and smelled her womanhood through the lace panties. It was a heavenly smell. He wanted to lick her there again. He could feel his arousal coming on.

"Continue." Denny said.

"*Votre chatte est brulante.* I love your …hot chocolate! It has a …rich aroma."

"No, master," Elizabeth protested and tried to kick and shake him away as the script instructed.

Darcy held her legs and then took the feather duster from her hand. He traced the duster over her creamy flesh where it was exposed by the corset, then moved slowly down the front of her body and past her apex to the insides of her thighs.

The slow ministration made Elizabeth moan aloud and abandon her struggle.

"Now you're all clean for your master," Darcy said, and moved up over her as if to mount her body.

"*Il y a du monde au balcon,* wench. Don't pretend. I saw you… peeking at me when I took my bath, last night." Darcy said.

"I couldn't help myself. You have the sexiest body," she murmured.

"Call me Master." Darcy then smacked her hip lightly.

"Master, you have the sexiest body."

"So you admit to wanting me, wench?"

"*Oui,* monsieur."

Darcy then imitated the thrusting actions, burying his face against the deep V of her bodice.

"Hey are you two professional porn stars? How come the moaning and screaming were so boring? Move over Darcy, let me demonstrate!" Denny said.

His words prompted Darcy and Elizabeth to moan and scream loudly, exhibiting more passion as the fake thrusting actions began to excite them both. Luckily for them, only a few minutes passed before Denny called "Cut!", signaling the finish of the role-play.

***

Watching, Darcy and Elizabeth recalled how, at the end of the filming, they had breathed a sigh of relief, collected their normal clothes, uttered a hurried goodbye and scrambled out of the suite.

When they reached Darcy's room, he slammed the door shut and said, "*Repliez sur la table.*"

Elizabeth eyes widened, "You want to continue the role-play?"

"Bend over the table, wench, or you will be up for punishment. Do as I say!"

"*Non, monsieur,*" Elizabeth winked and protested. Darcy turned her around and bent her over.

"*Ouvrez vos pattes!*"

"*Non, monsieur!*" She was determined to defy his order.

Darcy smacked her bottom and said, "Open your legs, wench!"

"Ouch! That hurts!" Elizabeth continued to protest, still refusing to obey.

"Then you will be punished for the entire night for disobeying your master. "

He used his knee to nudge her legs apart. His hands squeezed and cupped her breasts through the corset. He then freed his arousal, pushed her lace panties aside and thrust into her hot, wet womanhood from behind. Their coupling was intense and loud. And again they forgot protection.

They didn't come out for dinner that night. The French maid costume and feather duster proved very useful.

Darcy said a few times *"Votre chatte est brulante"*, or your pussy is hot in French, throughout the night. He liked to drink her hot chocolate, and he dusted her down with the feather duster even more thoroughly...

***

Darcy and Elizabeth were roused from their reverie about the steamy night they'd spent by admiring whistles from the audience in the studio. It seemed the clip of their role-play had ended and the audience had liked it quite well.

***

So, who won the Challenge and two days of relaxation on another deserted island?

Richard and Charlotte. They earned many points from the judges, who thought the water-gun shooting sequence was hilarious.

And who lost?

Surprisingly, not Collins and Caroline. It was Charles and Jane. It seemed that their role-play was neither hot enough nor funny enough, as compared to others. They were treated to the final torture of a painful full-body waxing (with their swimming costumes on).

But what happened to our favourite couples?

Georgiana made her way back into Darcy's good books by arranging for Elizabeth and him to go off to Fiji without Collins and Caroline.

From there, they traveled back to Boobie Hill, where Darcy stayed on his 'parole' for a week. Then after three months of long distance romance, Elizabeth moved to Sydney. She rented a small apartment and worked in a travel agent. Their romance continued.

Darcy finally managed to persuade her to move in with him, five months later. Then six more months passed before she said yes to his marriage proposal. The High and

Mighty Darcy Junior didn't make an appearance for yet another year, But the happy couple then had three more children. Not surprisingly, the nerdy scientist was extremely diligent in his research, planning and implementing an endless array of sexy games and role-plays to spice up their matrimonial love lives.

Bingley and Jane flew to Sydney after Fiji, where she stayed there for three months before tying the knot. They had two children together.

Richard and Charlotte carried on a hot affair for about three months before they drifted apart.

As for Collins and Caroline, they eventually each found other targets to stalk, after four years.

Why so long?

It's because *Sexpert Challenge* was a huge success for Lady C Productions. The show remained the top-rated program for Channel 12 over seven seasons. The saucy format and the successful romances of Bingley and Jane, as well as Darcy and Elizabeth, all contributed to the success of the show.

As for Collins and Caroline, they both gave up their old jobs and became an 'odd couple' who were invited to many comedy shows and events. They were so busy with their appointments that they didn't have time to stalk.

One thing that continued to make Elizabeth and Darcy uncomfortable, however, was that every time they encountered Caroline, she would hint that Darcy had strange tastes in women, at which point she would attempt to console Elizabeth privately.

And what about our famous TV-industry couple? Lady C was very satisfied with Wickham's performance, both on- and off-screen. She kept him with her for many years. But as she grew older, she became increasingly interested in S&M. Wickham tried to leave her several times, but his spending habits and sexual proclivities had become so dependent on her that he had to return, each time, after a few months of straying. In the end, he became the most infamous 'boy toy' in the industry.

What if Mr. Darcy was a foul-mouthed chef?

CHARMERS IN THE WALLET

"Jane, I want you to raise your bloody voice and give Lydia the shit! She's late and she's lazy. She cooks the crappiest oysters I've ever eaten. She skips out of the kitchen and flirts with all the male diners. Longbourn Restaurant will not survive another six weeks if you don't begin acting like a boss," Charles Bingley yelled at the top of his voice.

His furious expression made Jane Bennet burst into tears. She pulled open the back door and ran out of the kitchen.

He hurried after her. "Sorry, sweetie!" he called from the doorway. "I didn't mean it. It's only written in the script. You know Darce. He's the opinionated one here. Jane, wait!" Charles took off his microphone and chased after her.

"Follow them!" Darcy yelled at the camera crew, then muttered, "Great!" sarcastically to himself and stormed off to the walk-in pantry to cool off, "Now we've lost the cast. I don't want to be stuck here! I'll die of frustration."

He sat down on a barrel of olive oil and dropped his head into his hands. He loved food and he loved the walk-in pantry. As a boy, he had often hidden in the pantry at Pemberley when he was chased by his cousin Richard.

Celebrity chef Charles Bingley was the face of "Heat Up the Kitchen Table," but he was not the foul mouth personality he portrayed in front of the camera, a larger-than-life character who helped restaurant owners around the world to rescue their businesses. In reality, he was the forever cheerful man who was renowned for indecision.

The format and success of the show were due more to its quiet and insightful producer, William Darcy. Darcy was a successful businessman and media mogul with an arrogant and perfectionist attitude. He had scripted many of the initial controversial confrontations on camera which had served to launch Charles and the show into fame and win the hearts of struggling restaurant owners.

The crew of the popular television show was filming in Meryton, trying to rescue a family restaurant, Longbourn. It had quickly become apparent that head chef Jane Bennet was a doormat who let her sous-chef and youngest sister Lydia trample all over her.

In Darcy's eyes, the mother and business manager, Fanny Bennet, was a nervous wreck who only wanted to marry off her daughters to any wealth patron who happened to pass through, and woman who should never have worked in a restaurant. She cried and screamed under the slightest pressure, as well as whenever she couldn't get her own way from her husband. The head waitresses, Mary and Kitty Bennet, were forgetful and slack. The father hid in the upstairs office with his books all the time – not accounting books for the restaurant, but books from his personal library on philosophy and history. No wonder the restaurant was in dire need of a rescue.

The only person worth a glance was Elizabeth Bennet, the second eldest daughter. Actually, she was worth many glances. She had dark, curly hair, intelligent, bright eyes, witty conversation and a lovely smile, not to mention a body perfectly suited to his taste.

Darcy would never understand how Charles could prefer the skinny, willowy type like Jane. He himself was definitely a 'meat' lover who liked his woman voluptuous.

But Elizabeth didn't work in Longbourn Restaurant. She was a chocolatier who owned and operated three shops called Pure Indulgence. Chocolate was Darcy's weakness. And he had soon discovered that *her* chocolate was pure heaven. She had been using her profits to subsidize the ailing Longbourn for the past year, and it was she who had written to "Heat Up the Kitchen Table" to ask the show to help rescue the restaurant.

Darcy had met with Elizabeth several times before the shooting was due to begin. It wasn't the norm, but Charles had fallen in love with his angel, Jane Bennet, immediately after meeting her, and so he had persuaded Darcy to come for the pre-show meetings in Meryton, where he spent hours monopolising Jane's attention while Darcy and Elizabeth were left to "entertain" each other. Darcy thought that Elizabeth liked him. She certainly seemed to like to get a rise out of him in a sweet, arch way, always arguing with him about this and that, although never flaunting herself. And he had certainly been getting quite a rise every morning since he met her. She had been featured prominently in different positions in his erotic dreams for days, now.

The problem was that no woman in London, or anywhere else, had held any interest at all for him, since then. To be honest, he hadn't been seriously interested in anyone since his father died. The occasional Friday night out wasn't worth a mention.

Elizabeth was different. She tempted him too much and too fast. But he was a billionaire businessman with a family who relied on him and a self-made fortune. He had been chased by the most beautiful women in the world for years. He would not act on his infatuation yet, particularly not with a woman who had such a troublesome family.

That was why he had delayed the shooting at the Longbourn Restaurant for almost five months, distracting Charles with other urgent projects. Two weeks ago, however, Darcy's and Elizabeth's paths had crossed accidentally. He was attending a food and wine function in Kent with his cousin, only to discover that she was exhibiting her chocolate creations there. She was as tempting as her Pure Indulgence. And that blasted Richard had used every possible minute to flirt and chat her up. Darcy was green with jealousy and almost tongue-tied, at first. But he drew comfort from the fact that she kept talking and teasing him, despite Richard's efforts to monopolize her.

Darcy now believed that Elizabeth still liked him very much, even after a five-month absence. Maybe she had been waiting for him to take the first move. So here he was, finally arriving with his crew to shoot the episode about Longbourn. He hadn't produced the series personally for a while, but he had come anyway. Two weeks on, however, he had seen her only once or twice. He hadn't had the opportunity to put things out in the open with her yet, but he was determined to do it soon. He had finally admitted to himself, just this morning, that he needed to make love to her soon or he would lose his insanity.

"Where the bloody hell are you, Darcy?"

Elizabeth's voice startled him from his reflection. He was about to reply when the pantry door was pushed open with such a force that the hinges nearly flew apart. He was confronted with the sizzling hot vision of the pocket-sized dessert goddess wearing a red, silky halter top and tight white jeans. *No wonder her chocolate sells so well. I wouldn't mind visiting her shop every day if she wears clothes like this while serving me.*

Darcy calmed his thoughts and spoke politely. "What can I do for you?"

Elizabeth walked a step closer to him, her hands on her hips. It was a most distracting sight for Darcy. As he was still sitting, his eyes were almost on the same level as her cleavage. And what cleavage! She was furious and breathing so hard that Darcy couldn't help hoping the seam of her top would burst.

"What can you *do* for me? Can't you wash your mouth out and rewrite your script for Charles a little bit more politely? Did you know that you had him saying 'Fuck you!' over 40 times in that script? Jane has a delicate heart, and she can't take all this foul language and yelling."

Lord, I'd love to fuck you too, again and again! Darcy thought. He was exhausted. He hadn't been able to sleep well for months now, due to the erotic dreams he was having about this woman. On top of that, the shooting hadn't been going smoothly, as Charles was too damn distracted by his angel. And now this woman was thrusting her breasts in front of him, invading his space with her sexy scent. He wanted to pull her onto his body and stop her yelling with violent kisses.

But he chose not to do that…yet. The pantry was not the right place.

Instead he replied politely again. "It's the truth. You want us here to rescue Longbourn, and we need her to act like a boss. Otherwise, there will be no Longbourn Restaurant any more."

"Can't you make the pill a bit sweeter to swallow? Do you have to ask Charles to swear every three minutes?"

"But that kind of television sells. I bet the footage with Jane in tears and Charles comforting her will shoot the ratings rocket-high."

Elizabeth was getting angrier and angrier. Her mom and younger sisters had been biting her ears off for bringing in this rescue team. Jane was under a lot of stress and avoided talking to her at all. Creditors were knocking at her door. She couldn't keep subsidizing Longbourn much longer. It might well sink her own shops, too.

She had come in to see the late-night shoot, just in time to see Jane run off in tears. Elizabeth's heart ached, and she was torn between running to comfort her or staying to read the riot act to the arrogant producer. She disliked Darcy all the more because, during their first meeting, she had overheard him telling Charles that she was so plain that she wasn't worth a minute of his time. Since then, she had delighted in teasing and making fun of Darcy, to get revenge for that conceited remark, even though she found him handsome, intelligent and business-savvy. And she hated him all the more after meeting him in Kent again.

When she'd seen Charles chasing after Jane, she'd decided to confront Darcy. She stepped closer still and almost breathed her words on his nose. "You're only interested in your show. You're a cheat! You don't care about any of the restaurants you promise to save. Bloody arrogant cheat! I'd have been much better off to hire a business coach to help us than getting us onto your rubbish show."

The one thing Darcy hated most was when people questioned his honesty. His blood boiled, and he stopped her from yelling at him in the way he had most been wanting to.

Surging to his feet, he used one hand to grab her by the waist and pull her close. She stumbled and fell heavily against him. With his other hand, he held her head and bent to kiss her violently. He poured all the frustration from his erotic dreams into the kiss. When he sucked on her upper lip, it tasted of pure dark chocolate. Then his tongue pried her lips open and thrust into her mouth, which tasted of hazel nut and milk chocolate. He rammed his tongue into her mouth, twirling, pushing, withdrawing, thrusting again and again, telling her silently how he wanted to possess her body.

Elizabeth struggled at first, trying to push away from him and stand on her own. But after his tongue invaded her mouth, she was lost. She wrapped her hands around his neck and ground her body against his. His six-pack muscles gave her the most stimulating sensation! Her nipples peaked and her stomach lurched.

His hands smoothed over her naked upper back and grabbed her bottom through the jeans, squeezing and rubbing her cheeks. She was much more responsive than in his dream He untied her top, then sank back into his chair and pulled her down onto his lap, reaching around her to plant his hands on her treasure mounds. They were firm and bouncy. Her skin was smooth and her nipples hardened like rocks.

He felt a huge arousal coming. As she rubbed her bottom over him, he nearly came in that instant. He tried to slow his body down, but her breasts were more than he could resist. He squeezed and fondled them with avid interest, making her moan and squirm on his lap.

The friction was too much. Maddened, he pushed her to stand up and rose with her, tearing at her jeans. He succeeded in opening them and forcing them, along with her tiny panties, down her legs.

Elizabeth gasped, feeling the cool air on her body. Inside, however, she was boiling and eager for action, too. She unbuttoned his shirt and kissed his hairy chest.

"You're the most arrogant person I know," she murmured against his skin as he caressed her mound, "but you're just piping hot!" She pushed her hands down his trousers and grabbed hold of his butt. Her fingernails teased the crest of the cheeks, sending shivers down Darcy's spine.

He abandoned his caress of her apex and tackled his trousers, pushing them and his boxers down in one go. Then he pressed her against the shelves, kissing her, kneading her twin peaks, rubbing his arousal against her, bombarding her with rich sensations all over her body.

"I want you. I can't wait!" He growled like a hungry lion, then pulled her legs up to wrap around his waist.

"Me either. I'm so hot!" Clinging to him, Elizabeth suckled his earlobe and dug her fingers into his back.

He supported her creamy bottom and teased his shaft against her entrance, not entering, just touching and opening her secret lips.

Elizabeth moaned aloud with the contact, and he echoed her. She was so wet that she could feel her essence flowing down her body.

Darcy was hard and huge, unable to bear another tease. He pushed his thick manhood into her, slowly at first because she was so tight and small. Inch by inch, his body invaded, sinking into her warmth.

Elizabeth was speechless and breathless. Darcy was strong and powerful in every inch of his body. He stretched her muscles and skin, on and on, conquering every pore and surface of her inner self. He was so slow and patient that she kissed him passionately to urge him on.

At that, he sensed her needs and thrust deep into her with one mighty final push. She screamed out loud, feeling a molten sensation in her core, as it had never been touched and stretched so deeply and intensely before.

Then, raising her, he withdrew almost his whole length from her before pounding into her again. His potent manhood warred with her soft, moist muscles. His hands manipulated her bottom as he slammed into her again and again. The friction, the wetness, the pounding, their moaning and breathing created an intense, erotic rhythm in the pantry. On and on, he thrust into her, until she felt as if her blood were boiling and radiating throughout her body. She felt weightless, shivering and convulsing as she reached heaven.

Her whole body went limp. He drove into her for a final few times and then he also lost control, trembling violently as his seed fountained up into her.

Then he sat back down on the barrel, with her straddled on his lap. The two of them still hugged each other tightly, enjoying the aftermath of their earth-shattering mating, with their bodies still linked together.

Slowly, a sense of reality returned. They were in the final stages of dressing in silence when Darcy suddenly blurted, "Shit! I forgot the condom."

Elizabeth pulled open the door and walked into the now deserted kitchen. The back door was locked, and the restaurant in the front was pitch black, the only light coming from the pantry.

She steadied herself against the kitchen table. *It's 2 o'clock in the morning!* He had been fucking her senseless for almost an hour. She was angry with herself for allowing him to make love to her without protection. He seemed to make her forget herself completely. She was supposed to hate him. "Luckily for you, I'm on the pill," she said tightly.

"There's still no excuse for me. But you're so hot that you make me forget everything." Darcy wrapped his arms around her from the back, kissing her neck tenderly.

She shivered and tried to turn away from him. "No need for flattery. I know you find me a 'plain Jane' who isn't worth a minute of your time."

"Shit! You overhead that?" He let go of her and raked his fingers through his hair in embarrassment. "I wasn't myself, that night I met you. I hadn't even looked at you properly when I said those words. But I was hooked on you before the night out."

She turned, craning her neck to look him in the eye. "But I hate you."

"Hate me? I thought you liked me."

"Arrogant, conceited man! Why would I like you?" She scowled up at him. "Richard told me you deliberately delayed shooting the episode about Longbourn because you wanted to separate Charles from the woman with the 'objectionable family.'"

"Fucking gossiping Richard! I'm going to strangle him, next time I see him."

"Do you deny separating Charles from Jane? She was heartbroken for months!"

"Richard got it all wrong!"

"But he talked about somebody being 'like a horny rabbit, wanting to fuck the woman senseless, every time he sees her.' And he said 'her mother and younger sisters were too much trouble, so he chose to delay shooting for nearly five months.'"

Darcy was furious with Richard. "I didn't use those vulgar words. And I wasn't talking about Charles and Jane. I was talking about you and me."

Elizabeth stared. "Shit! You've had the hots for me for that long?"

"I can prove it. I've condoms in my wallet." Darcy pulled out his wallet and slammed the condoms in different colours on the kitchen table one after another. "They are there to remind me that I've lusted after you for all these months. And I'll use all of them with you, all night long, if I can get my hands on you again, one day."

Elizabeth eyes widened on seeing the number of condoms he pulled out. His hands were braced on either side of the kitchen table, trapping her there. He was breathing hard, his six pack rising and falling rapidly.

He looked magnificent when he was angry.

"So…you didn't find me plain? And you didn't scheme to separate Charles and Jane?" she asked.

"No." He shook his head with vigour.

"Then what are you waiting for?" She wrapped her hands around his neck and tried to pull his head down for a kiss. "The condoms are waiting."

Darcy raised his hands and stopped her. "Actually, I've a different position in mind for each different-coloured condom." He then turned her around and pushed her to lie on the kitchen table, face down. He lowered his head and kissed her earlobes, neck and naked back, trailing hot, wet kisses over her body.

Elizabeth shivered. She felt chilled as the front of her body pressed against the cold stainless kitchen table. But she felt hot as his lips were scorching her back. Blood rioted in her body again.

Without further foreplay, he unbuttoned her jeans and bared her creamy bottom to his assault. He shoved his trousers down, pulled on the blue condom, joined her on the table and drove into her from behind with one mighty thrust.

Holding her hips, he thrust into her like mad. His arousal was hot and hard, slamming into her core, deeper and deeper. Elizabeth screamed and wriggled her bottom to meet him, thrust by thrust. Primed as they already were, their mating was rough, hot and fast, and they quickly reached a simultaneous climax.

Not long afterwards, they retired to Darcy's hotel to test out other positions and discuss strategy for how he could best handle her family. Both skipped work for the day, blissfully unaware of the firestorm of publicity that hit Longbourn when the restaurant's sous-chef, Lydia, reported to the police that a thief in the night had raided her kitchen, stealing two dozen oysters and leaving behind an unused silver condom on the kitchen table.

What if Mr. Darcy participated in another reality show?

DARCY AND WICKHAM SWAP PARTNERS

"Thanks for tuning in to Celebrity Dancing Shoes. Welcome to everybody in the studio and the millions of viewers at home! I'm Charles Bingley and this is my co-host, that elegant but annoying sister of mine, Caroline Bingley." Charles flashed a big grin at the camera, earning a smack on the arm from Caroline.

"Hello everybody! Just ignore Charles. He has grown up to be quite silly. I'm sure you're all familiar with the format of our highly successful show as it enters into its fifth season. We take celebrities who have had no formal dance training and pair them up with professional dancers. Over the course of ten weeks, the celebrity has to learn ballroom, Latin and several other forms of dance. Each week, during our live broadcast, one couple is voted off, based on a combination of the scores they received from the judges and the votes they received from the viewing audience. If the scores are tied for two couples, the one with more audience votes wins."

"Tonight is our final competition of the season. In Week Eight, there were only two couples left. Our first gentleman is William Darcy, a very good friend of mine. The world-famous artificial-heart inventor pairs up with waltz champion Ann de Bourgh. The money raised from your votes for him goes to the Heart Foundation."

Caroline said, "And George Wickham, our home-grown Bollywood heartthrob, unfortunately pairs up with British rumba champion Eliza Bennet."

"Why 'unfortunately'?" Charles asked. "Elizabeth is beautiful, talented and hot!"

"Which is unfortunate for all of our female viewers at home," Caroline explained, "since Miss Eliza has put her hands all over George's body for so many weeks. The viewers, I'm sure, would like to trade places with her. And George's charity is 'No More Bullies.'"

"Darcy has a lot of female fans out there, too," Charles stated, rallying for his friend. "Although the judges have said that he learned and executed the techniques of every dance very well, they do agree that he has been too uptight, not showing any emotion when he dances with Ann. As a result, he hasn't been receiving very good scores from the judges. Week after week, I've expected him to be voted off, but my handsome friend must have thousands of female fans voting for him, because he's still here tonight in the final."

"As for George and Miss Eliza, they have been leading every week," Caroline noted with a dazzling smile for the camera. "His dancing techniques are not as precise as Darcy's, but George is more entertaining and charming on the dance floor, and he matches well with Miss Eliza."

Charles held up a cautioning finger. "But our 'devil' judge, Frederick Wentworth, said on Week Seven that he sensed that George's 'sincerity' might well be fake, and he believed that there was tension between the partners. And he gave them a very low score of five."

"That sent the gossip magazines and talk shows into a frenzy," Caroline added smugly. "Everyone heard, at the beginning of the series, that Bollywood George seemed to be very taken with Miss Eliza. He has been seen visiting her home in Meryton, taking her to nightclubs and, in fact, leaving her place on a few early mornings in 'not so tidy' attire. In fact, I recall a headline from a gossip magazine during Week Five that claimed that Miss Eliza was caught buying a home pregnancy test kit. It read, 'Small-Town Hoofer Preggers by Bollywood Bad Boy!'"

"Caroline, I'm sure that was pure gossip!"

"Was it?" Caroline held up a colorful tabloid magazine. "Here's a headline from Week Seven, when Miss Eliza was said to have come out of a local clinic with tears in her eyes. 'Dumped Dancer Seeks Abortion.'"

Outraged by Caroline's deviations from the script, Charles deftly changed the subject. "Then both couples should thank our producer, Jimmy Forester, who has introduced a fate-turning twist. We announced two weeks ago that the remaining couples would switch partners for the final two weeks of the competition. Darcy is now paired up with Elizabeth, and Ann with George. Let's roll the camera and see our new couples in training."

In the first film clip, a hot and flushed Elizabeth, who had apparently just finished a training session, was interviewed by Caroline. The latter was dressed impeccably in an orange princess dress accentuated with a multicolour silk scarf and a two-storey hairdo.

"How lucky, Miss Eliza! You got to pair up with William and even stay as a guest at Pemberley, his impressive country estate, for two weeks. How did a small-town girl like you fare? I image his ballroom is bigger than your entire house. I hope you didn't get lost in the corridors."

"There are a lot of lovely trees, flowers, birds and small animals on the grounds here. I love being able to lose myself in Nature when I finish a day's training."

"Miss Eliza, we saw your shocked reactions when we announced the switch of dance partners. Was it because William was heard saying you only had a 'tolerable figure' and that your mother was 'coarse and mercenary'?" Caroline asked, her tone snide.

"Oh, did Darcy say that? Remind me to introduce him to my uncle. You could say that he is even more 'coarse and mercenary' than my mom, Since he is in the gold mining industry," Elizabeth replied, and grinned.

She then added in a serious but sweet tone, "I've been training with George for eight weeks. Naturally, I wanted to complete the competition with him and win the trophy. I was just shocked with a swap so late into the series. I'm a professional, though, and I'm sure I could teach even a skeleton to dance well." Gossip magazines often laughed at Caroline, saying that she walked and danced like a skeleton dipped in orange paint because she was so thin, behaved so arrogantly and wore orange clothing all the time.

"Oh, you wanted to win the trophy with George? How touching! Then the off-camera rumors must be true. Are you pregnant?"

"You seem awfully interested in home pregnancy kits, Caroline..." Elizabeth winked while Caroline's face turned deadly red. "As for me, I only went to the pharmacy to buy high blood pressure pills for my mom. Perhaps you need some? You look quite red now. Maybe you have high blood pressure, too."

The footage stopped there, and the studio audience broke into a fit of laughter.

Charles couldn't help but laugh, too. Then he continued, "The gossips did absolute wonders for our ratings. Last week, we did a recap of our couples' journey to the Finals, to allow our newly formed couples two weeks of bonding time, and over 5 million viewers tuned in to watch."

"Here is some further footage from that two weeks of intense training," a red-faced Caroline said, when cued by the production team. She would kill Jimmy after the show. She had specifically asked him to cut out that "high blood pressure" footage.

Now, on camera, Pemberley's ballroom appeared, where a casually dressed Darcy met up with Elizabeth. He looked serious and pensive.

"Miss Bennet. How do you do, today?"

"Hi, Darcy. Why so formal? I've seen you frequently over the past eight weeks. Even if you won't call me 'honey,' like George does, I'm sure you can do better than 'Miss Bennet,'" Elizabeth replied teasingly.

She had also known Darcy socially for the last few weeks, as her sister Jane was dating his good friend and host, Charles. She had also learned about how he had mistreated George, regarding an inheritance from Darcy's dad. George also said that Darcy was a playboy with a number of kept women. As a result of that, along with his remarks about her figure and her mom, she found him arrogant and conceited, and enjoyed taunting him, every opportunity she had.

"They may be filming us secretly now," Darcy said.

"Why should you be afraid to get comfy with me in front of the camera? We have to dance a rumba together during the Finals. You know that the rumba is a sensual dance. It should be like making love with me in front of the camera, so you'd better get used to it."

"I'm not very good at this – at being comfortable with women," he said, and blushed.

"Really? Just imagine that I'm your lover number 18."

"What?"

"Just something George said… That you had gotten comfy with quite a number of women."

Darcy's eyes shone with anger. He said coldly, "George is vulgar and a bad influence, Miss Bennet. I hope you haven't paid too much attention to what he's said, and that you haven't slept with him, as the gossip magazine claimed. I would also hope…"

Elizabeth grew angry, too, and suddenly pressed her body into a surprised Darcy. She wrapped her arms around him, positioned her hands on his butt and smacked him with force. "Okay, Mr. Gossip, let's concentrate on our job. Here is Lesson One on how to touch your partner, rumba style," she said archly.

The footage stopped and Caroline cried out, "Scandalous! No wonder some gossip magazines claimed that Miss Eliza was a …"

"Wow, Caroline," Charles interrupted hastily, "do you think our sly producer has any more secret footage to show us before the dances begin?"

The light in the studio dimmed, and the announcer said, "Dancing the rumba certainly is like making love! So let's see if William Darcy really can make love with a stranger…in a sensual rumba."

Standing in the centre of the darkened studio, Darcy trembled when Elizabeth wrapped her arms around his back and pressed every inch of her body to his. The music began, and she smoothed her hands down his back as she swayed her body down at the same time, leaving absolutely no space between them.

He felt like he was being electrocuted. The sensation of having her hot breasts drawing a zig-zag path from his chest to his belly, and down to his thighs was beyond words. He hoped he wouldn't have an erection in front of millions of TV audiences. He told himself to remember the routine...but all he could remember was the previous night.

What had happened last night?

When he'd first met Elizabeth at the launch of the season, he hadn't paid much attention to her. She wasn't an eye-catching blond like her sister Jane...but he couldn't help noticing that she danced with passion, even partnered with a low-life like Wickham. After her dance routines, Elizabeth's eyes would shine and glisten. A lovely crimson colour would blossom under her creamy skin. Her breasts would seem about to burst through her tight top, as if begging for a squeeze. Her butt and thighs were tightly toned, ripe for fondling. And, best of all, she would smile and laugh with joy, as if she had just successfully completed the world's most difficult challenge.

Darcy had wanted to write her off as a loser who only wasted her life partying away, but then he began to encounter her frequently at social functions with Charles and Jane. He soon learned that she was, in fact, a dance teacher and a nurse.

She was witty, intelligent and independent. In fact, she was altogether different from the fake women who frequented the 'old money' circle. She didn't need plastic surgery or high fashion to enhance her beauty. She didn't need a rich man to satisfy her shopping or spending needs. He particularly admired her sincerity and her loyalty to Jane, their family and her friends.

He felt it was rotten luck that she had gotten herself entangled with Wickham. Darcy was strongly attracted to her, and she was off limits to him, not least because he didn't want to be Wickham's successor, thereby giving Wickham a chance to gloat.

In the two weeks since switching partners, Darcy had been in big TROUBLE. He had the hots for Elizabeth, and it didn't help that she was staying at Pemberley, with her room only a few doors from his.

He could feel her soft curves, and inhale her fragrant lavender scent and spicy hot breaths during rehearsals. Scene after scene of sexual fantasy flashed through his mind, and he was in a constant state of arousal, day and night. That was why he had chosen to wear loose trousers all the time, excusing his awkward walking to all the dancing practice. He had been like a zombie, with no thoughts except those about her hot body.

Darcy, extremely embarrassed, was sure that Elizabeth knew about it, because she had to touch his body during the dance. Since he was seriously distracted by his sexual fantasies, he didn't learn the routines and techniques as quickly as he had with Ann. That frustrated Elizabeth a lot, and she increased their hours of training from six to sometimes as many as ten hours a day.

The long sessions and constant nagging from Elizabeth finally got to Darcy. After training from 8 am to 4 pm non-stop the day before, Elizabeth was still not happy with his performance and wanted to extend the training till 7.30 pm, right before dinner. But he couldn't bear the tension of holding her body for another second. He refused, stomped his foot, stalked out of the grand ballroom and shut himself up in the library.

Elizabeth decided to let him cool down. Around 7 pm, however, she was determined to talk to him again and to persuade him to put in two more hours of training after dinner.

She knocked on the library door with an 'I'm the teacher, and so you had better behave' expression on her face.

After several knocks, he still hadn't responded. She was getting pretty worked up, and she banged even more loudly on the door.

Bang! Bang!

Her fist was raised in preparation for banging on the door the third time, and so she was unprepared when it opened and she suddenly came face-to-face with a muscular bare chest. She couldn't hold back her hand.

Bang!

She left a red mark on Darcy's naked torso.

"What the hell?" He felt the pain and growled.

Embarrassed, Elizabeth wanted to apologize but, hearing his growl, she couldn't resist defending herself. Slipping past him and kicking the library door shut to prevent others from hearing their argument, she yelled back, "You brought that on yourself! You left the training like a spoilt child and then refused to open the door when I knocked nicely."

His eyes widened. He couldn't believe she was blaming him when she was the one who had smacked him.

"I was asleep, you crazy woman! I didn't hear your knock, at first. And I didn't leave the training like a spoilt child. I left after 8 full hours." Raising his hand to his left chest, he massaged the flesh where her fist had landed, then turned slowly and walked to the couch at the far right-hand side of the room.

It was Elizabeth's turn to widen her eyes. She had seen many bare-chested men on beaches before, but his shoulders were broad and muscular. His chest was smooth except for some hair near his belly button, tapering down to disappear into the waistband of his black –

— *underpants! He's only wearing underpants!* Elizabeth thought, panicked. Words tumbled out of her mouth.

"You're the crazy one! You've danced with me for two weeks with your erection pressed against me the whole time. Luckily, the TV crew was only there for one day to shoot our training. And now you open your door to me in your underpants. Are you a pervert?"

Darcy froze in his path towards the couch and wheeled to look at her. She was standing there, legs apart, hands on hips, her lips opened as her face turned red. His sleepy head cleared abruptly, for Elizabeth's pose looked somehow familiar to him. Pictures raced through his mind, and he suddenly made the connection. *Yes, from my Internet research about how to tell whether a woman is interested, this surely is an aroused woman!* He became aroused immediately, happy that Elizabeth had the hots for him, too.

"There you go again!" Elizabeth took a step forward to scream right into his face. "Can't you get one of your women to keep your little Willie down, at least for a few minutes? We have a dance competition to win tomorrow. I don't want my reputation ruined by your animal insti…"

He had had enough of her accusations. He pulled her by the waist, closing the gap between their bodies. Then he mashed his lips against hers to silence her. He poured all his weeks of admiration, lust and frustration into the kiss, biting her lips and thrusting his tongue into her mouth.

At the same time, his hands were busy branding her body. First, her tight butt needed fondling. The thin cotton of her dress was no barrier. Secondly, he ran his hands down her thighs, feeling their strength and smoothness. Then he freed one hand to cup her breast. It was pert, the perfect size for his big palm. When the contact caused her nipple to harden, he couldn't help but pinch it, while his other hand pushed aside her G-string so that he could slide his fingers in to trace her secret lips.

Elizabeth's hands came to wrap around his neck. *Good, she likes it – no resistance.* He slipped one finger into her entrance. It was tight, and she threw back her head, giving a loud moan.

Feeling her legs begin to buckle, he picked Elizabeth up and placed her on the large couch, which he had had custom-made to fit his six-foot frame. To his satisfaction, there was plenty of room on it for the two of them.

Elizabeth was in a haze. She didn't understand why she wasn't protesting. She didn't like him at all. He was a known womaniser! But he was also handsome and intelligent, nothing at all like George, who talked non-stop about his famous and exciting career. He didn't talk much, most of the time, but when he did, he expressed the most fascinating and fresh ideas about medical issues and the care of patients. His hands and tongue were like magic bands! Maybe two weeks of non-stop sensual dancing and living together had muddled her head, too.

Thinking back to the *Is she interested in you?* research, He followed its advice and pushed down the spaghetti straps of her cotton dress, baring her wonderful breasts. Thrilled by the sight, he suckled and squeezed her nipples.

Elizabeth felt a hot flush race through her body and moisten her G-string.

Continuing with his experiment, he pushed the skirt of her dress up to her waist and hastily pulled off her G-string. He devoted one hand to the continued worship of her breasts while he moved down to enable his lips to settle on the curls at the apex of her thighs. He breathed in her scent, and found that it was heavenly and utterly unique.

When he parted her thighs more widely and lowered his head to trace his tongue along her entrance, Elizabeth felt torched by fire. She arched her back, offering herself.

His hand left her breasts and moved down to part her secret lips. He thrust his tongue in and out, tasting her.

It was too much for her. Within a few scant minutes, she screamed in ecstasy and came.

He raised his head from her womanhood and stripped out of his underwear, then lowered his body onto hers, chest to chest, hips to hips. "Look at me, Elizabeth. I want to be inside you now. I've been thinking of this moment for weeks."

She tried to fix her gaze on him but she was still on her high and couldn't concentrate.

He kissed her mouth and stroked her breasts while he slowly pushed the tip of his erection against her wet entrance and then rocked his hips, entering her. That brought Elizabeth back from the other world. His manhood was so much thicker than his finger or tongue! She felt as if her insides were fully stretched, and the feeling was unbelievable. He was very hard and yet irresistibly smooth, creating a strong, silky friction deep inside her body.

He reached down to raise her feet to wrap around his waist. Then he pushed hard into Elizabeth, all the way to her womb. He closed his eyes and let his body savor the sensation. He was tightly enwrapped, intimately squeezed. Blood seemed to have stopped flowing to his brain, intent instead on shoot through other regions of his body like heated missiles.

His body was on automatic pilot. He thrust in and out of her, again and again. His hands pleasured her breasts. His mouth danced a tango with hers. He lost track of time until the missiles burst from his body, flooding her with his seed. Then he collapsed on top of her.

When he finally returned from heaven, he clasped her tightly, then rolled onto his back, moving Elizabeth on top of him. Only then did he notice that she had tears on her face.

"Oh my god, did I hurt?"

"It hurt at first. You're a big man."

"And then?"

"And then what?"

"Did it still hurt after the 'at first'? I'm so sorry – I was concentrating on getting to the heaven myself and I don't even know whether you came or not." He was embarrassed. His research had warned that men should give pleasure to their women first.

"You have a one-track mind!"

"Sorry. Researchers are like this. So?" He urged.

"So what?"

"Did you come?"

"I screamed."

He looked stricken. "Did I hurt you that much?"

"I twisted my body until it ached."

"Oh, that sounds bad! Did you want me to stop earlier?"

"My body felt torched by fire."

"Damn!" He felt terrible about hurting her. He covered his eyes with his hand and wished he could bury himself in a hole.

"And then I had a huge climax that went on and on," Elizabeth whispered.

He dropped his hand and stared at her. "Are you teasing me, woman? I thought you didn't come."

Heartened, Darcy was ready to roll her over to "punish" her again. But he saw that she had fallen asleep. Carefully, he slid from beneath her and got to his feet, gazing down at her in wonder…then froze when he saw that there was blood on her bottom.

Hurrah! She never slept with Wickham, after all, Darcy thought. Then a new thought struck him. *She was a virgin and I didn't use any condom! We may have created a child.* Mental images of little boys and girls with his unruly hair and Elizabeth's glistening eyes running wild on the Pemberley grounds flashed through his mind.

Good! Tomorrow after the competition, I'll ask her to move in with me, and we can get married soon afterwards.

Then another picture forced its way into his mind. He imagined hearing a high-pitched voice at his dining table – Elizabeth's mother. She was talking about marrying off her younger daughters to his rich cousins or friends. Meanwhile, Elizabeth's younger sisters, done up in trashy outfits, were flirting with all of the male members of the party.

All right then, he decided, *no one from her family except Jane will be allowed to attend any of our gatherings.*

He shuddered at the thought of Elizabeth's coarse family members, and the involuntary movement startled Darcy out of his gloomy reverie. Aware again of his dark studio, he looked down at Elizabeth's sleeping form and whispered aloud, "Let's win this competition…and then we will have to talk."

***

"Well now, William and Elizabeth, your hair and makeup are done, so I'll leave you for half an hour to rest and talk about the strategy for your next dance. No one is allowed to disturb you. There are some sandwiches here, if you'd like them. Then, at 8.45, I'll come back with the costume team to help you get ready for your freestyle dance. Just make sure you don't mess up your hair and makeup in the meantime. By the way, congratulations on earning four 9's with your rumba!" With that, Louisa Hurst, the production assistant, shut the door and left them alone together.

Darcy saw a high-spirited Elizabeth turn in her chair. With glittering eyes, she said, "That was a great performance! You finally nailed it."

"Finally, we have a moment to ourselves." He left his chair, knelt in front of her, took her hands and said, "Frankly, Elizabeth, I liked the private dance we did last night on my couch even better. Our rumba just now has left me hot and unfulfilled."

"You've got nerve mentioning last night!" she said, and he felt her trying to pull her hands from his.

"Why not? You and I both enjoyed it. We could relive it right now, you know."

He lowered his head and meshed his lips with hers before she could say another word. He parted her lips with his tongue and traced her inner mouth thoroughly for several minutes. He liked the fact that her trembling tongue was playing duels with his.

His hands pushed the bathrobe aside and bared her shoulders and creamy breasts. His mouth reluctantly left her sweet lips and moved down to her delicious breasts. He laved and suckled one hardened nipple while his hand pinched the other one hard.

"Don't!" He heard her moan.

"Too painful?"

"We shouldn't be doing this. Someone may come in."

"We have half an hour to ourselves. Louisa said so." He stood up and turned away to lock the door.

When he turned back, he saw that Elizabeth risen, too, and turned her back to him. In the mirror on the wall, he saw that she had casually pulled her bathrobe up to cover her breasts, but not all the way up onto her shoulders.

"We shouldn't be doing this," he heard her whisper.

He walked back, wrapped his arms around her waist, pressed himself against her back and traced wet kisses from her earlobe to her neck and down to her bare shoulder. Then he untied the sash of her bathrobe. His hands cupped, weighing and rubbing her breasts eagerly.

He felt her shiver, and he looked into the mirror. His dark hands were a startling contrast to the snowy white skin of her breasts. Her lips were swollen by his kisses. Her eyes were heavy-lidded, half shut. The long hair piled on top of her head was in danger of falling down. This image of a sensually rumpled Elizabeth sent him into full arousal.

He pushed her bathrobe down to pool at her feet. Then, impatiently, he got rid of his. Looking into the mirror, he devoured her with his gaze, from her tiny belly button to the lush triangle at the apex of her thighs.

One of his hands left her breast and traced a hot path down her belly. "This is sweeter than last night. I didn't get to look at your lovely body before you slipped out of the library," Darcy signed.

Suddenly, he felt Elizabeth tremble. She turned and wriggled out of his touch.

"Damn! What are we doing here? Put your bathrobe back on!" she demanded breathlessly. Crouching down, she picked up her bathrobe, pulled it on and moved behind a chair.

"What's wrong, Elizabeth?" Reluctantly, he also picked up his bathrobe and put it on.

"Everything is wrong!"

"Why?" Walking near her, he tried to take her hands. "I thought we had something really good going on here. I want you to move in with me after the competition."

She stared. "You want me to move in with you?"

"Yes! I want us to get – "

"You're disgusting! You want to know what's wrong? I'll tell you what's wrong! I gave my virginity last night to a womaniser who is arrogant and conceited. He cheated a childhood friend out of his multi-million dollar inheritance. He likes to look down his nose at family and friends whom I love a lot, even with all their faults. I just now nearly let him fuck me in a TV studio which may have cameras hidden somewhere. And now, he wants me as his live-in play thing!"

"Why are you so interested in George? He's a low-life."

"Oh yeah? Well, you're high and mighty! I just hate rich men who use their power and position to strip away other people's rights."

"Rights? His rights? Why do I've to listen to this crap?" He walked to the door, unlocked it and was ready to storm out when Louisa burst in with three girls from the costume department.

"What have you two been doing? I told you, no messing up the hair and makeup!"

"We were ... practicing our freestyle," Elizabeth and Darcy replied in unison, then glared at each other.

***

It was 3 in the morning. Darcy watched Elizabeth leave the after-show party. He'd noticed that, like him, she hadn't had much to drink, the whole night. He followed her at a discreet distance.

Luckily no one delayed his departure. She was heading towards the garden of the hotel, not back to her room. The garden was deserted, and she settled on a bench at the farthest end, behind some trees.

Summoning his determination, he approached and said quietly, "Miss Bennet, sorry to disturb you."

She stiffened in surprise. "What do you want now?"

"You hurled some serious allegations at me, earlier. I would appreciate a chance to defend myself."

"Allegations? They were the truth."

"You have already listened to Wickham. Wouldn't it be unfair not to listen to me, as well? I thought you were a defender of people's rights."

She glared at him, but she kept her silence. He took it as a sign to continue.

"Wickham is the son of my dad's Personal Assistant, and he's a year older than me. My father was very fond of him, from the time he was born. When his father died suddenly when he was ten years old, their family was in a bad shape. Dad settled them in a cottage within Pemberley. George and I played together when we were young.

"My father paid for his education at a boarding school and later in university. When my father died, ten years ago, he left a piece of property in Brighton that Wickham would inherit when he turned twenty-five. Dad also left Wickham a senior position in our family business, Pemberley Finance, if he wanted to work for us.

"My Uncle Andrew was the executor of the will. Wickham approached him and said that he didn't want to wait four more years for the property, nor did he want to work for us. Instead, he wanted to become an actor and move to Hollywood, and so Uncle Andrew settled with him the market value of the property and the equivalent of four years' wages in the position he could have had in Pemberley Finance. All in all, George was handed more than five million dollars.

"He went to Hollywood then. Within a year, though, he'd spent all of the money. Then he came back and demanded more money and a job in Pemberley Finance. Uncle Andrew refused.

"It seems that my uncle learned that Wickham had been quite wild since his late teens, partying, drinking, doing drugs and gambling. My father and I didn't know much about that, at the time. Wickham must have gone to great lengths to hide his bad habits from my father, during his lifetime. And since I had become obsessed with medicine by the time I turned thirteen, I didn't know about George's excesses, either.

"After Uncle Andrew refused his demands, Wickham disappeared from our lives...until last year. That's when my younger sister went on a three-month cultural exchange program in Mumbai. She met Wickham there. Apparently he had gotten himself established in Bollywood.

"Georgiana, who was sixteen at that time, had been very fond of Wickham when she was young. She was soon persuaded to Wickham's version of events, and she dated him for several weeks. One day, unannounced, I flew to Mumbai to surprise her. I arrived at her apartment and found that Wickham – that low life – had tied her to the bed, naked, with a camera rolling. He and a co-star were trying to...to force themselves on Georgiana.

"I've never felt so violent in my life. I nearly killed both Wickham and the other bastard. Only Georgiana's crying stopped me. I smashed the camera and kicked them out. They hadn't succeeded with their evil deed, but Georgiana felt utterly broken. She couldn't sleep, couldn't bear to go out of the house. She had hideous nightmares every night for over six months."

"Oh my god! Did you report it to the police?"

"Georgiana couldn't face it. She begged me to take her back to Pemberley immediately. She said she had already slept with Wickham a few times, and so she was afraid, if we reported it to the police, that Wickham would claim that she was just a rich, spoilt brat who wanted to capture a threesome on tape. She didn't want to risk facing such humiliation."

"How is she now?"

"These past six months, Georgiana has been doing much better. She has gone back to school and is spending the summer holiday with my cousin Richard."

Elizabeth stared at him intently. "Then what George said about you being a womaniser...that must be lies, too!"

He could feel color suffusing himself, but he met her gaze as levelly as he could and answered, "I had never been with a woman, before last night. I didn't even know how to tell whether you'd had an orgasm, that first time. I'm so awkward and stupid in these things.,,"

"What? Are you telling me that you were a thirty-year-old male virgin? That can't be true! Not in this day and age!"

"I know I'm... weird." He swallowed hard. "But I was... traumatised by Wickham when I was thirteen."

"That bastard! What did he do to you?"

"I can't... tell you. I'm sorry. It's just too painful to talk about. But the result was that I swore off of girls and women during my teenage years, when I should have been lusting and chasing after them. Then I discovered my passion for research. My mom... died slowly of heart failure. I saw her fade away over a two-year period. I wanted so badly to find a way to replace her heart.

"Even now, I seldom go out to social functions except fund-raising events for the Heart Foundation and the annual dinners of Pemberley Finance. Uncle Andrew and Cousin Richard take care of the business. On those occasions, I ask my cousins Ann, Sophie, or Cassandra to go as my partner. I only agreed to this show because Charles said that I could use it to raise people's awareness of heart disease by talking about it in front of millions of TV viewers, rather than burying myself in research.

"I'm uncomfortable around strangers, especially someone as... expressive as your mom and younger sisters. I did say to Charles that your mother was coarse and mercenary, and that I'd prefer not to spend too much time with them. I apologise for that. I now know that I should learn to be comfortable with your family, because I...I want to have a life with you.

"When I asked you to... move in with me, I was thinking of that as our next step towards marriage. After all, we didn't use any protection. You could be... pregnant."

"Marry me? Are you crazy? We haven't even gone on a date!"

"True, but you said yourself that we had been seeing each other frequently for the past weeks. You always challenged and taunted me. And you gave your first time to me. I thought that meant that you loved me as I love you."

"How can you love me? I'm just a nurse in a small-town hospital, a nurse who happens to love to dance. You're a world-famous artificial-heart inventor, with money to burn."

He shook his head in stubborn negation. "You're witty, intelligent, loyal and hot, entirely different from the fake women in the old-money circle. I was... attracted to you almost from the very beginning."

"But you said I only had a tolerable figure!"

"That was... before I had really looked at you. Not many days after I said that, I found that I was fantasising about your body. I had so many erotic dreams about you that I started to conduct some research..."

"Research? On what?"

"On how to tell whether a woman is interested in you," he said, pausing a minute before he continued. "Anyway, it seems that the information I gathered from the Internet was wrong. I'm sorry that I misunderstood you. Thank you for listening to my explanation."

Darcy stopped again. He wanted Elizabeth to refute him, but she didn't say anything, continuing to scowl at him. He swallowed the lump in his throat and said, "Will you at least promise to tell me if you discover that you're pregnant?"

"I've been on the pill for months, to control my irregular periods."

His heart squeezed. He supposed he should be relieved, but he wasn't. He found that he could barely mask his disappointment and sadness. There wouldn't be a little boy or girl with his unruly hair and Elizabeth's glittering eyes after all. "Oh! Well then, I won't... take up any more of your time, then. Goodbye, Elizabeth. Thank you for coaching me for the past two weeks, and for choreographing two brilliant dances. I'll treasure the memory of these two weeks forever."

He turned and walked back to the hotel. He had hoped she would stop him but she just sat there, not even saying goodbye to him.

***

A week had passed: 7 days, 168 hours or 10,080 minutes without Elizabeth. Darcy shut himself in the library. He wasn't doing any research. He was simply spending every possible minute on the couch. He wanted to breathe in the remains of her lavender smell. He wanted to relive the moments when he was enwrapped and squeezed hard.

He also watched the recording of their two dances together, over and over again. He loved the rumba because

Elizabeth was willingly touching every inch of his body. He could still remember her breasts tracing a dangerous path from his chest down to his thighs. Then she had moved to his back, using her breasts to draw another zigzag path from his shoulder blades down to his bottom, sending shivers through him.

After that, it had been his turn to smooth his hands all over her body, from her shoulders down to her ripe bottom. Then, turning her around, his hands had smoothed their way up from her thighs to her taut belly to the sides of her breasts.

Afterwards, their bodies were pressed together, chest to chest. He pulled her right thigh up to his hip by bending her knee. It was strongly reminiscent of the position in which they made love. Afterwards, she'd wrapped her hands around his neck while he pulled her clinging form around the dance floor. It was an erotic, sensual dance, like the mating of a loving couple.

The freestyle had been entirely different. He now understood why Elizabeth had choreographed such a dance. It was a reflection of her dislike of him. It started with a tango and ended up with a samba. First, Darcy tried to court Elizabeth in a nightclub setting. She slapped him on the face and they engaged in a hot, high-tension tango well-suited to their true feelings at that time, for they had still been angry with each other about what had happened during the break. The fight in the tango was a furious exchange reflected in their eyes, facial expressions and body language. They tore their Latin costumes to pieces in the process.

Elizabeth was left in a samba bikini with glistening fringe, and he was in a tight, sleeveless T-shirt and shorts as the tango music faded, giving way to a samba rhythm.

Seemingly tired from their fight, he sat down on a chair. Elizabeth jumped onto the one opposite and shook her generous breasts, creating a waterfall with the fringe, taunting him. Every time he shook his body samba style on the chair and pretended to kiss her breasts, she moved just out of his reach.

Elizabeth jump up from the chair and danced around the perimeter of the dance floor. He chased after her in samba moves, then pretended to slip and laid half down on the floor, still shaking his body. She came back to him, placing her feet on either side of him, then shaking her body fiercely while she moved all the way past his thighs, his waist, his chest, until she stood over his head. Half-reclined on the floor, shaking samba style, he eyed her glittering body at close range...

Watching the video, he could still remember with exquisite precision how his body had shivered when he saw her sex passing so close above his mouth. He had longed to lick her. It was a raunchy moment of erotic tension between two stubborn lovers, each of whom wanted to win over the other.

Finally, he jumped up, chased her down, and scooped Elizabeth onto his shoulder, positioning her face-down, bottom-up. He was supposed to smack her lightly to end the dance but, a bit angry, he had smacked her bottom with more force than necessary. The music stopped. The dance was over.

With applause ringing in his ears, Darcy turned her away from the camera and gave her bottom a hard squeeze before he put her down. After he released her, she had glared at him the whole time as they received their scores and won their trophy.

He had just finished watching another round of the recording when he heard a knock at the door. He didn't bother to get up from the couch. He simply called, "Come in."

The door opened and Elizabeth, dressed in a long dark windbreaker and high heels, came in, shut the door and locked it.

Am I hallucinating? He wondered wildly, and jumped up to stand beside the couch. He was bare-chested, wearing nothing but underpants that sported stains from where he had gratified himself while he watched the recording. "Elizabeth!" he croaked.

"William, I..."

"Don't say a word! Let me find my jeans and T-shirt first." He hastily pulled on his clothes, tidied his hair with an unsteady hand, sat down behind the massive desk and gestured Elizabeth to sit in the chair in front of it. "Now, what can I do for you, Miss Bennet?"

Taking her time, she sat down. Then she squared her shoulders and said, "You were very unfair, the other night in the garden of the hotel."

Darcy's heart fell. He'd held onto a tiny hope that she had come for another reason.

"Unfair? How?"

"I let you talk, uninterrupted. But then you walked away before I could say my piece."

"You have more to say about my failings?"

She bit her lower lip. "Not yours, but...the low-life's."

"Did he do something bad to you, too? I should have killed the bastard in India, while I had the chance!" He jumped up from his chair, came around the desk, paced two steps towards Elizabeth and stopped. Then, with a sigh, he went back to sit down behind the desk. "Sorry, Miss Bennet. Please continue."

"The gossip magazines were right."

"But you didn't sleep with him."

"No, it wasn't me. But he was sleeping with Lydia, my youngest sister. I introduced them, just two weeks into the show. He got her pregnant. I blamed myself, and I bought the pregnancy test and checked out the clinics for her."

"But Lydia was only 15 years old. Did you report it to the police?"

"Lydia said no. She said she loved him. But the bastard denied responsibility and said he didn't know how many men she might have slept with, before and during their time together. In the end, she miscarried."

"That was why there was so much tension between you two, towards the end of the season."

"Yes. I asked Jimmy Forester to let me pull out, to say I was ill or had a dying relative. Of course, I couldn't tell him about Lydia. I just said flatly that I couldn't dance with George anymore. Forester said he would think about it, and then he pulled the partner swap trick. I think he believed that the low-life was sexually harassing me, and that he would be less likely to do so with Ann."

"But why did you defend Wickham then?"

"I didn't. I just don't care for your high and mighty attitude."

He dropped his gaze from Elizabeth's tense face and looked down at his hands, feeling that all hope was gone. *She never liked me at all.*

"It was a brilliant trick. It did wonders for the ratings." He said dully, fighting to retain his self-control, holding onto whatever topic was available. He barely notice when Elizabeth stood up and walked towards him.

"Just good for the ratings?" she whispered in his ear.

Darcy was caught off guard. He automatically pushed himself and the chair sideways, moving away from Elizabeth...but also inadvertently opening his thighs for her to move in and stand between them. Reluctantly, he looked up.

She smiled down at him, tender and teasing. "Didn't you like the switch in partners?"

"Mmm..." He wasn't sure how he should answer. He didn't want to anger her with any stupid words from his mouth while she was smiling.

"Didn't you like our samba?" She pulled her iPhone out of the pocket, pressed a button and placed it on his desk. As samba music filled his ears, Elizabeth untied the sash of her windbreaker and pushed it off her shoulders to reveal a yellow samba bikini with glittering beads and fringe.

Darcy's eyes widened and his jaw dropped. He was having trouble breathing.

He watched as she put her hands on top of her hair. She began to wiggle her breasts in front of him in a rhythm that bewitched him. She then took one of his hands and placed it on her cleavage.

He felt the earth move. His hand got to touch her creamy breasts again and again as she shook them for him. She continued to dance, moving forward toward the junction of his thighs.

He felt his arousal stretching his jeans. He wrapped his free arm around her waist and pulled her body against his, stopping her dance. His head now joined his hand, resting on her breasts. He breathed in deeply, absorbing her lavender scent.

"You don't hate me anymore?" he asked, and raised his head to look her in the eye.

"I never hated you," she said softly. "I told myself that I didn't like you...but after you were gone, I stayed in the garden for a long time, thinking about us. I admitted that you were handsome, hot and intelligent, even on the night we made love. I don't believe I would have slept with you if I weren't attracted to you. Then you explained everything to me about the low-life and about your…awkwardness."

Hardly able to believe what he was hearing, he said, "Why didn't you let me know earlier – that night? Or this past week? I spent 10,080 minutes without you, and I was in despair!"

"I had to work out my feelings. And I was waiting for you to come back to me again."

"But you refused me. I thought you would want me to respect your decision. And I…I was afraid of more rejection."

"But I'm afraid, too! You're a handsome, incredibly rich man. I worried that, after a few days, you would come to your senses and wouldn't want to bother yourself with me."

"Never! You're a beautiful, hot, talented woman. I don't understand why you were still a virgin at 22."

"I was too busy with dancing and studying. And a lot of the men in Meryton thought that John Lucas, my dance partner, was my boyfriend. Actually, he's gay. And then, when I was partnered with Wickham, he just seemed too…smooth."

Darcy found that he could breathe again. "I'll have to thank John, the next time I see him, for helping you save yourself for me!" Lowering his head, he licked her cleavage.

That made Elizabeth moan.

He stood up, picked her up, swept the paperwork from the desk and laid her upon it, her legs dangling over the edge. He parted her thighs and leaned his body on her, then asked, "What are we going to do now?"

Her eyes sparkled. "You're going to make love to me on your desk. Isn't it obvious?"

"Well, yes. But I mean, are you going to be my girlfriend or something?"

She arched her eyebrows playfully. "Let me think! I'll give you an answer after I score the performance you're going to give in the next few minutes." She flashed him a brilliant smile.

"In that case, I'll implement one of the findings from my recent research." His hands palmed her breasts and smoothed over them in a circular motion, making her nipples harden…but the beads and fringes were a hindrance. He fumbled and searched. "Where have you hidden the clip?"

"On the back."

Darcy put his hands underneath her and tried to open the clip. He couldn't see where it was, so he rolled her over onto her stomach.

She put her elbows on the desk, trying to turn her head to see how he was doing.

"This opening mechanism is more complicated than a car engine!" he grumbled.

"I've every confidence in your ability to persevere."

"Finally!" He flipped open the clip. "I swear that I'll invent a simpler opening for a bikini top."

He was about to roll her over onto her back again, but then he was distracted by her glittering bottom. It made him remember the final move of their freestyle, When he'd had her on his shoulder. He felt a sudden urge to smack and squeeze her bottom again, preferably naked.

Undress her, man!

He pressed hot kisses on her neck, then down her spine. In one swift movement, he stripped down her bikini bottom and tossed it over his head, baring her delicious derrière.

She gasped.

He gave her a playful smack on the right cheek.

"What are you doing?" Elizabeth demanded, glaring at him over her shoulder.

He gave her another soft smack on the left side.

"William!" she scolded.

He parted her legs, lowered his mouth and kissed her inner thighs. Her bottom shook and wiggled on the edge of the desk. He then slid a finger into the secret of her sex. It slipped in easily, for she was already wet. He slid another finger in while tracing her secret lips with his thumb, and Elizabeth trembled.

"Oh, William," she moaned loudly.

He pushed both fingers in and out of her, slowly at first, then increasing the pace. He saw her arch her upper body, and felt her inner muscles contract just before she cried out. Her elbows sagged, and she let her upper body sink back onto the desk.

Darcy pulled out his fingers, moved his hands to pull her upper body up from the desk slightly, then squeezed and massaged her breasts while he pushed his thick manhood into her from behind with force.

"Oh yes, William!" she screamed.

It was heavenly. He closed his eyes for a second and savoured the feel of her tight, wet muscles around his manhood. When he opened his eyes, the sight of their naked bodies joined together aroused him further. He felt his sex grow even larger inside her.

He saw her arch her upper body as she held herself up with her elbows and turned slightly to watch him. Her eyes were half closed, her lips parted, and her breathing had become shallow. He shifted one hand from her breasts and held her hip, while his other hand continued to pleasure her twin peaks. He pulled his manhood nearly out and pounded into her again with force.

The samba music played on, a musical incitement to riot.

He stayed inside her for a moment, grinding his tip against her womb, then pulled nearly out and thrust hard into her again. Her breasts shook with the rhythm of his pounding.

Their moans and screams became louder and louder. He felt her muscles contract around him in a wave of tremors, and couldn't control himself any longer. His body shivered and bucked, and he spilled his seed into her, then collapsed onto her back.

After recovering for a few moments, he said smugly, "Hello, Miss Judge. What is the score for my performance?"

"Mmm… a seven."

"Only a seven?" He had hoped that he would earn a 10 and convince her to become his girlfriend, his lover, his wife and, soon, the mother of his children.

Heartbroken, he pulled himself out of her and collapsed into his chair, his whole body sagging.

He sensed her turning to look at him, but he was too depressed to respond. He heard her cross the space, and then he stiffened in delighted surprise as she sat on his lap. "Of course a seven," she murmured sweetly. "You will need years and years of my private training to improve enough for me to award you a perfect 10."

"You teasing woman!" He wrapped his arm around her waist and gave her a tender kiss. "So, you *are* my girlfriend now?"

"Yes."

"Will you move in with me?"

"My suitcase is outside."

"Will you marry me?"

"Maybe, once you've improve on your skills enough to get an eight," she said, and laughed.

"And that would take how many years of training?"

"Oh, at least until I reach twenty-five."

"But that's three years away. Please, Elizabeth, no more than a year. Don't you know that, according to research, the earlier you become a mother, the smarter and healthier the babies will be? "

"You talk too much about research! Just shut up and kiss me."

***

In the end, they got married after two years of living together. Each year, they celebrated the loss of their virginity in the library with new dance moves. Even their four children were not allowed to disturb them on such nights.

As for the scores, Elizabeth never once awarded him a perfect 10 during their fifty years of marriage. She said it was important for a truly dedicated student to keep learning.

Darcy branched out in his inventions, not on simpler bra clips, but with ideas on how to help nurses and doctors to better care for their patients. Pemberley Inventions, when floated in the London Stock Exchange, was a huge success.

What if Mr. Darcy was a difficult boss?

AMATEUR EROTICA

Bloody arrogant pig! Elizabeth Bennet swore under her breath and saw her boss of six months walk out of the office.

Mr. William Darcy is the most arrogant jerk in the universe! she swore again.

He had demolished her hard work of an entire week in just a few minutes, criticising the design as 'dull' and 'boring'.

It's now nine o'clock in the evening, and she vowed not to waste another second slaving for him.

On the deserted office floor, she knew the best way to vent her anger. She called up her story folder, typed in the password and started writing.

> Who does he think he is? W.D knows nothing about me. I confess I've feasted on the sight of him, time and time again. His physique is that of the ideal male model: six feet four inches, broad shoulders with hard biceps. His bottom is perfect

and his thighs muscular. The curly hair on his chest goes wonderfully with his perpetual tan. His unruly hair begs to be ruffled. His eyes are dark and intense, and his lip begs to be passionately kissed.

He told a friend that I was a prim and proper spinster, a dull and boring secretary who did his bidding well enough, but that he wouldn't take me out to a function. I might blend so well with the white wallpaper that people would bump into me without even noticing.

I've had enough of his vicious tongue. I've planned my revenge. This is the big day. He has instructed me to stay behind to work on an urgent project.

I'll let him see just how prim and proper I'm—not! Since I'm only five feet two inches in height, there's no chance for me to succeed with this revenge unless I use drugs, so I went to the pharmacy and bought a packet of travel sleeping pills.

It's near eight o'clock, and the office is deserted. He asked for coffee to be brought in. "Immediately!" He used his clipped tone, as usual. I cut one pill open and put a quarter of it into his coffee cup. I don't want him to be unconscious for too long. I made the coffee the way he likes it, then stirred it frantically.

When I brought it in, I waited for him to drink it all while I kept busy around the files near the corner of his office. After a few minutes, I could see his eyelids slowly closing. I couldn't suppress the smile on my face. I danced out of his office and went to my desk to retrieve my bag.

Then I walked back into his office, locked the door and pulled him down from his chair onto the floor, ever so carefully. I didn't want to injure him. He needs to be somewhat conscious when I deliver my revenge.

I took out the ropes from my bag and tied his ankles to the legs of the desk. Then I raised his hands above his head and tied them to the legs of the couch nearby.

Now that I had him positioned as I wanted, I took out a pair of scissors to cut up his Armani suit jacket and trousers, and the Ralph Lauren's shirt. You needn't be alarmed. I'm not a psychotic woman. I wouldn't use the scissors on W.D's cock or his beautiful body. But I enjoyed every minute of shredding those hateful clothes which made him look like a Greek god every day.

By the time I had him down to his underwear, he was starting to wake up. I could see his sinfully long eyelashes batting. Then his eyes opened and he looked groggily around.

He tried to move his legs and then his hands.

He raised his head and had a look at his body.

"What the fuck are you doing? Untie me immediately!"

"You'll only hurt your wrists if you pull like that again," I said sweetly.

"Then untie me this instant, Beth!"

"Not until after I've my revenge."

"What revenge?"

"You told Binkley that I'm too prim and proper, dull and boring."

"You are! Look at your clothes. You're buttoned up to the neck, black on black, without even a necklace or earrings to break the monotony."

"You'd better shut up." I held up the scissors and smiled at him menacingly.

He clamped his mouth shut and looked at me with the first trace of fear.

My heart laughed but kept my face expressionless. He didn't know that I only intended to cut off his remaining underwear.

I knelt down besides him and did just that. Hmm, he really is like a Greek god, very well endowed. I had only ever been with a couple partners before, and W.D. from this angle looks huge, even though he's not aroused at the moment.

Then I stood up. Put the scissors away and started to undress myself. I did it slowly, intending to tantalise him.

First, I shrugged off my serviceable jacket. Then I hooked a finger on its collar, walked near him, swayed it along his chest and circled it around his cock.

Ah, he loved the caress. His arousal sprang up immediately.

I tossed away the jacket and took off my shoes. Then I started unbuttoning my black shirt, starting at the neck, while I used one of my bare feet to trace a line along his thigh.

I could see the vein on his leg pulsing, and his shaft grew larger.

When I took off the shirt and revealed the leather-laced corset underneath it, his eyes nearly popped out.

I moistened my lips. "Do I look prim and proper now?" I asked in a sultry voice.

"Take off your skirt and I'll let you know." That was his coarse reply.

"Arrogant pig!" My eyes flashed with anger, and I used my toe to stroke his balls.

He gasped and panted.

I didn't obey his order but unlaced the corset instead. Once it was off, I started fondling my breasts seductively.

His gaze followed every movement of my hands. He swallowed hard, and his cock stood up even straighter.

Only then did I unzip my skirt, wiggle my butt and let it pool at my ankles.

His pupils dilated and his hands balled into fists upon seeing me with garter belt and stockings only.

"Yes, I never bother with underpants." I took the pin from my hair and shook my unruly mane to life. Then I walked near him, stepped over him with my right foot, and slowly lowered my body to sit on him.

He raised his head as my breasts neared, clearly wanting to taste my nipples.

I straightened slightly, not allowing him to lick them.

"Do you like the feel of my stockings?" I rocked my body forward and backward, letting him feel the texture of my stockings.

"Your pussy feels better than the polyester."

"Pig!" I might not be rich but I paid tons for my sexy lingerie. His foul mouth needed punishing. I grabbed his shaft and gave it a hard squeeze.

He yelped, but I couldn't be sure if it was from surprise, pain or ecstasy.

"I'm a stud, not a pig," he retorted through gritted teeth.

I burst out laughing. "Whatever you're, you'll beg for mercy." Shifting position, I lowered my head and swallowed his rod. When I started swirling my tongue around it with vigour, he raised his hips in helpless thrusts and came within minutes.

His seed was hot and salty. He had such abundance that it overflowed from my mouth.

While he lay panting hard on the floor, I went to his mini bar and took out a bottle of chilled champagne.

I flicked a few icy drops onto his manhood. He sucked in air. I poured some more, washing away his cum. He gasped again as the cold liquid struck his hot flesh.

"Beg me to stop!" I commanded.

He bit his lip and refused to comply.

"Stubborn bull!" Well, I wouldn't waste a whole bottle of quality champagne on his cock. Raising the bottle, I drank from it thirstily as my hand kneaded his rod with rough force.

After a few minutes of loud moans and cries, he came again. This time, his seed spewed everywhere, spattering onto my breasts and stomach.

"Ah, two orgasms in such short successions. Is that a record?" I asked.

His eyes had rolled back as if he was dead. "Yessss." He whimpered the word out.

"Well, let your dull and boring Beth take you to new heights." I poured the remaining champagne over my breasts, allowing it to wash away his hot fluid. Lowering my upper body over his face, I teased his mouth with them.

At that, he came back to life, his lips parting to take in my nipple. His tongue wetted and teased it, sending hot blood rioting through my body.

I raised my bottom and slid my wet pussy along his shaft. His limp cock twitched once, twice, and then jerked upward, abruptly rigid. I didn't hesitate, impaling myself on him with force.

Ah!

Ah!

Both of us cried out loudly as we joined together. I lowered myself, engulfing him to the hilt, my body stretching to the maximum. I had never experienced the invasion of such a thick, hard cock before. After all, he's more than ten inches taller than I am, and his shaft was undoubtedly the largest I had ever fucked.

My wet inner muscles felt torched by fire. Like the detonation of a bomb, heat burst into my womb, and my body felt torn open by his rod.

Our skin pulsed together. It took me several minutes to absorb the physical and emotional impact of our union.

He bit his lip, thrashing beneath me, then cried out, "Fuck me hard!"

I had no qualms about following his order, this time. I raised my butt and then pushed down onto him, hard and loud. He thrust up, as well, matching my rhythm, bucking like a wild stud determined to throw me. Like a crazy rider, I rode him in a frenzy. My fingertips dug into his chest as I impaled myself on him again and again.

Every time his tip pierced the opening of my womb, I squeezed his rod and hips more tightly. My nails scratched at his torso. When we finally came together, my pussy was flooded with his burning seed.

After Elizabeth finished the violent erotic scene in the story, she saved the document, switched off her computer and went home.

The next day, when she returned to work, she found that Mr. Darcy was acting oddly. He seemed to stare at her, more and more openly. For the past six months, Elizabeth had worked with the man for many hours in the office. She also knew him socially, since her sister Jane was dating his best friend, Charles Bingley.

He never spoke much about personal matters during those social occasions, but he did engage with her in heated debates about everything and anything. And he glared at her frequently, but nothing like today. She could feel him gazing at her breasts and bottom, following her body movements. He wandered in and out of her office for no reason at all, and he called her into his office more often than usual.

By five o'clock, she was more than ready to call it a day and leave. But a last-minute summons from the great man meant she was in for another round of work.

By eight o'clock, the office was deserted. Her concentration on the current design was broken by the buzz of the intercom.

"Miss Bennet, please come into my office." His deep voice seemed laced with menace.

Elizabeth bit her lip and replied, "Yes, Mr. Darcy."

She straightened her pencil skirt, tidied her wayward hair with an extra pin and walked into his office.

He looked at her without a word for a long while. Then he stood up, turned the monitor towards her and said. "Please explain to me what this is." As Elizabeth advanced towards his desk, he moved away and walked to the door.

When she saw the file open on his computer, her mouth gaped open. It was her erotic story. How had he found the folder and cracked her password?

The click of the lock made her whirl around.

"What are you doing?" she asked shakily, seeing that he was removing his suit jacket.

"What you wanted me to do." He walked towards her, dropping his jacket on the floor. When he reached her, he picked her up and sat her squarely on his desk.

"You don't understand. It's just a story," she protested, gobsmacked as he unbuttoned her jacket.

"You're Beth and I'm W.D. What's so hard to understand?" He breathed in heavily, then kissed her hard.

When he thrust his tongue into her mouth, she surrendered. Drawing back, she admitted having been attracted to him for a long time, despite his demeaning words about her appearance and his constant criticism of her work. Then she kissed him back passionately.

When they came up for air, he explained quickly, "I've always found you very handsome, handsome enough to tempt me. My initial comment to Charles was just a ruse, to cover up my over-enthusiasm for your alluring body. I was hypercritical of your work because I was frustrated every time I came near you."

Her eyes widened. "You're interested in me?"

"I've been having steamy dreams about you for nearly six months now."

"And I've written over 400 pages of erotica about you!" she confessed, and blushed crimson.

"I don't like your story one bit."

"What?"

"My hands were tied in your story. I prefer this." Darcy used his strong hands to tear open her shirt, sending buttons everywhere. "What? No leather-laced corset today?"

She licked her lips and shook her head. "But I can wear one next time, if you ask nicely."

He flipped open her front-clipped bra, and her lush breasts sprung free, as if begging for his attention.

He squeezed one, and the nipple puckered, tall and hard. He lowered his lips to kiss it. Then he licked and suckled it, as his other hand plucked the twin peak.

Her body felt weak. She used her hands to support herself on the desk as her head lolled backward.

Suddenly, his hands abandoned her breasts and parted her legs.

"Don't wear a pencil skirt in future!" he demanded huskily.

"What do you know about women's skirts?" she panted.

"A-line skirts are my preference." He pushed her tight, narrow skirt up to her waist and pulling her towards the edge of the desk. "Hmm, no garter belt. And why the underpants?"

"I might be persuaded to leave them at home if you ask nicely," she said, provoked.

He grinned, showing his lovely dimples. "But you don't like me being nice." He tore off her underpants roughly and then unzipped his trousers.

She looked at his arousal with wide eyes. "You really are huge."

He laughed heartily, then spread her legs wider. As he lowered his head to kiss her mouth, he plunged into her hot sex with one mighty thrust.

Her arms weakened as she savoured the force of his burning shaft. She slowly reclined on the desk. His mouth didn't follow her. He used his palm to fondle her pert breasts, pushing, stroking, brushing and stimulating the creamy globes. His hips thrust in and out, forward and backward. His mouth gave out the sexiest moans and cries of ecstasy as his hard shaft created sparks inside of her.

His pounding didn't stop until she finally succumbed to the hot waves of arousal inside her body and screamed out as she reached climax.

It took her a few minutes to return to earth. She could feel his arousal, still big and hard, deep inside her.

"You didn't come?" she whispered.

He wiped a bead of sweat from her forehead and said, "I wanted to please you."

She didn't know what more he could do to please her. She had just experienced the most amazing, most mind-blowing orgasm her body could create.

But she was about to be proven wrong.

Darcy withdrew from her, picked her up and lowered her carefully onto the floor. Then he flipped her over, so that she knelt on all fours. With skilful hands, he worshipped the gorgeous twin globes of her behind, then reached beneath her to tantalise her breasts, rousing her from her satiation.

As her breath became shallower and her body tingled with anticipation, he pounded into her from behind. One hand slid from her breast to her satin belly, and then to her swollen apex. Using his fingers to rub her bud in front, he pushed into her from the back at frantic pace.

She was once again encountering an out-of-body experience. His strong, muscular body was touching her in places and ways that she had not been touched before. Their hot, sweaty bodies rubbed together. Her moans were echoed by his.

Her inner muscles were stretched and smarted, near their limit. Her thighs were forced wide by his. Elizabeth was nearing her peak, but this time she was determined to bring him with her. She squeezed him tightly, every time he plunged into her to the hilt.

Finally she couldn't hold out any longer. Her soul flew off to the sky as her body shuddered in ecstasy – and felt him come violently, as well. His whole body was fitted tightly into hers as he shivered and trembled, spurting his seed into her body again and again with explosive force.

The feeling was beyond words. Her erotic hero on paper was nothing compared to Mr. Darcy in real life. He was like a sex god, existing purely for Elizabeth's satisfaction.

What happened after that day? Elizabeth still wore a tight pencil skirt, serviceable bra and plain underpants to the office. And he tore several of them nearly to shreds during their late-evening office interludes, which lasted for nearly a month. Luckily, Darcy foresaw such events and stocked plenty of pretty replacements for her in his private closet.

She abandoned the 400 pages of erotica and concentrated on her real-life sex god for the rest of her life, achieving four children and countless mutual orgasms about which she could boast with him, in delicious privacy.

THE END

Made in the USA
Las Vegas, NV
02 November 2024

10732965R00135